DONNA GRANT'S
best-selling romance novels

"Time travel, ancient legends, and seductive romance are seamlessly interwoven into one captivating package."

—*Publishers Weekly* on Midnight's Master

"Dark, sexy, magical. When I want to indulge in a sizzling fantasy adventure, I read Donna Grant."

—Allison Brennan, *New York Times* bestseller

5 Stars! Top Pick! "An absolute must read! From beginning to end, it's an incredible ride."

—*Night Owl Reviews*

"It's good vs. evil Druid in the next installment of Grant's Dark Warrior series. The stakes get higher as discerning one's true loyalties become harder. Grant's compelling characters and continued presence of previous protagonists are key reasons why these books are so gripping. Another exciting and thrilling chapter!"

—*RT Book Reviews* on Midnight's Lover

"I definitely recommend Dangerous Highlander, even to skeptics of paranormal romance – you just may fall in love with the MacLeods."

—*The Romance Reader*

Don't miss these other spellbinding novels by
DONNA GRANT

CHIASSON SERIES
Wild Fever
Wild Dream
Wild Need
Wild Flame

DARK KING SERIES
Dark Heat
Darkest Flame
Fire Rising
Burning Desire
Hot Blooded
Night's Blaze
Soul Scorched

DARK WARRIOR SERIES
Midnight's Master
Midnight's Lover
Midnight's Seduction
Midnight's Warrior
Midnight's Kiss
Midnight's Captive
Midnight's Temptation
Midnight's Promise
Midnight's Surrender

DARK SWORD SERIES
Dangerous Highlander
Forbidden Highlander
Wicked Highlander

Untamed Highlander
Shadow Highlander
Darkest Highlander

ROGUES OF SCOTLAND SERIES

The Craving
The Hunger
The Tempted
The Seduced

SHIELD SERIES

A Dark Guardian
A Kind of Magic
A Dark Seduction
A Forbidden Temptation
A Warrior's Heart

DRUIDS GLEN SERIES

Highland Mist
Highland Nights
Highland Dawn
Highland Fires
Highland Magic
Dragonfyre

SISTERS OF MAGIC TRILOGY

Shadow Magic
Echoes of Magic
Dangerous Magic

Royal Chronicles Novella Series

Prince of Desire
Prince of Seduction
Prince of Love
Prince of Passion

And look for more anticipated novels from Donna Grant

Soul Scorched (Dark Kings)
*A Dark Kiss (*Reaper*)*
Moon Bound (LaRue)

coming soon!

WILD FLAME

A CHIASSON STORY

DONNA GRANT

Wild Flame
© 2015 by DL Grant, LLC
Excerpt from *Soul Scorched* copyright © 2015 by Donna Grant

Cover design © 2014 by Leah Suttle

ISBN 10: 1942017197
ISBN 13: 978-1942017196

www.DonnaGrant.com

Available in ebook and print editions

GLOSSARY

Andouille (ahn-doo-ee) & **Boudin** (boo-dan)
Two types of Cajun sausage. Andouille is made with pork while boudin with pork and rice.

Bayou (by-you)
A sluggish stream bigger than a creek and smaller than a river

Beignet (bin-yay)
A fritter or doughnut without a hole, sprinkled with powdered sugar

Cajun ('ka-jun)
A person of French-Canadian descent born or living along southern Louisiana.

Etoufee (ay-two-fay)
Tangy tomato-based sauce dish usually made with crawfish or shrimp and rice

Gumbo (gum-bo)
Thick, savory soup with chicken, seafood, sausage, or wild game

Hoodoo (hu-du)
Also known as "conjure" or witchcraft. Thought of as "folk magic" and "superstition". Some say it is the main force against the use of Voodoo.

Jambalaya (jom-bah-LIE-yah)
Highly seasoned mixture of sausage, chicken, or seafood and vegetables, simmered with rice until liquid is absorbed

Maman (muh-mahn)
Term used for grandmother

Parish
A Louisiana state district; equivalent to the word county

Sha (a as in cat)
Term of affection meaning darling, dear, or sweetheart.

Voodoo (vu-du) – New Orleans
Spiritual folkways originating in the Caribbean. New Orleans Voodoo is separate from other forms (Haitian Vodou and southern Hoodoo). New Orleans Voodoo puts emphasis on Voodoo Queens and Voodoo dolls.

Zydeco (zy-dey-coh)
Accordion-based music originating in Louisiana combined with guitar and violin while combing traditional French melodies with Caribbean and blues influences

PRONUNCIATION:

Arcineaux (are-cen-o)

Chiasson (ch-ay-son)

Davena (dav-E-na)

Delia (d-ee-l-ee-uh)

Delphine (d-eh-l-FEEN)

Dumas (dOO-mah-s)

Lafayette (lah-fai-EHt)

LaRue (l-er-OO)

ACKNOWLEDGEMENTS

A special thanks goes out to my family who lives in the bayous of Louisiana. Those summers I spent there are some of my most precious memories. I also need to send a shout-out to my team. Hats off to my editor, Chelle Olson, and cover design extraordinaire, Leah Suttle. Thank you for helping me get this story out!

Lots of love to my amazing kiddos - Gillian and Connor. Thanks for putting up with my hectic schedule and for talking plot lines. And a special hug for my furbabies Lexi, Sheba, Sassy, Tinkerbell, Diego, and our newest rescue - Sampson.

Last but not least, my readers. You have my eternal gratitude for the amazing support you show me and my books. Y'all rock my world. Stay tuned at the end of the story for the first sneak peek of *Soul Scorched*, Dark Kings book 6 out June 30, 2015. Enjoy!

Xoxo
Donna

CHAPTER ONE
SEPTEMBER

Nights off were one of his simple pleasures. Christian blew out a breath as he put his truck in park and slid out of the seat. Shutting the door behind him, he looked at the sign that read Joel's Place.

Normally, he would spend his night off at home. But since the house he shared with his three brothers now also had their women, he preferred some time alone.

Christian walked to the building and opened the door. He was immediately blasted with music and laughter. Stepping inside, he let his gaze wander the place. It might be his night off, but he was a Chiasson, which meant he was always working. The supernatural never took a day off.

He made his way to the bar and ordered a beer

as he continued to survey the people. Ghosts, demons, vampires, witches, werewolves. If they preyed on the innocent, then the Chiassons hunted – and killed – them.

His family had been protecting the parish for generations, and thanks to his brothers finding love, that would continue with future generations.

Christian's thoughts went to his sister, Riley. She was supposed to get out of the life. Not become a hunter. It's why he and his brothers had all agreed to send her away to college.

But they should've paid more attention when she called. Should have picked up on the clues. Riley was a Chiasson to the core. Stubborn, independent, and determined. She was no longer in Austin, Texas. No longer safe at school. And that fact worried Christian as nothing else could. Riley was smart, strong, and beautiful, but she also had a habit of being in the wrong place at the wrong time.

Their family had enemies. Enemies who had already tried to kill them.

"Hey," Sherriff Marshall Ducet said as he took the seat next to Christian.

Christian nodded in greeting. "You really come here often?"

"Yeah." Marshall looked around and shrugged. "It's a nice place. No...unwanteds here."

Marshall was a transplant from New Orleans. He'd left the city to get away from the supernatural, only to land himself smack in the middle of one of the other places in North America they all flocked to.

"Plenty of pretty women," Marshall said, wiggling his eyebrows.

Christian glanced at the two women shooting pool who kept eyeing him. They were attractive. Either one would do nicely as his bed partner for the night.

Emphasis on the night. Unlike Vincent, Lincoln, and Beau, Christian would do whatever it took to ensure that he didn't fall in love.

Ever.

"One for each of us," Marshall said.

Christian snorted. "Find your own. Those two are mine."

"You're a braver man than I if you want to take two women to your bed."

"What's the matter, Marshall? Worried you couldn't please both of them?" Christian asked as he turned his head back to the sheriff.

That's when his gaze snagged on a vision with pale brown curls that fell past her shoulders. She was wearing a white shirt that showed off her bronze skin and dipped low enough in the front to give a glimpse of cleavage.

Christian leaned to the side to see more of her and took in her faded jeans and cowboy boots. She waved at someone, and Christian quickly followed her line of sight to see one of the female bartenders return the wave.

Curls smiled, her face lighting up as she walked to a barstool and sat at the corner of the bar, giving Christian a perfect view of her.

His body responded instantly, causing his balls to tighten in need. Christian brought his beer to his lips and drank deeply as he took in her oval face and large eyes. Unfortunately, the dim lighting of the bar prevented him from seeing the exact shade.

With her full lips, delicate jaw, stubborn chin, and slender neck, Curls wasn't just pretty – she was intriguing.

"Ah, I see someone has caught your eye," Marshall said.

Christian pulled his gaze away from the woman. "Just checking things out."

"Right. Adding another to your stable?"

Curls was the kind of woman he would want all to himself. No sharing there. "Yep."

Marshall snorted. "Want to play a game of pool?"

"Sure." Christian took another drink of beer and spun around on the stool to follow Marshall.

Marshall racked the balls while Christian set aside his beer and grabbed a cue stick. Fate had brought Marshall into their lives, but Christian was glad they had someone they could trust in a seat of power.

Few people of the parish actually knew what Christian's family did, but there were some that joined in on a hunt when needed. Though the majority didn't have a clue that the Chiassons had saved their hides on multiple occasions, they seemed to realize the brothers were dangerous.

Dangerous didn't even begin to cover what they were. What kind of man brought a woman into such a family with the constant threat of death? His brothers might be willing to do it, but not him.

He remembered all too well his mother's murder and his father's death all those years ago. Those memories were enough to ensure that Christian remained alone. There was little time to protect everyone in the town. Why would he add a wife and children into the mix?

Only an idiot would do that.

His brothers, obviously, were idiots.

"Any word on Riley?" Marshall asked as he leaned over the pool table to line up his shot.

Christian waited until Marshall broke the balls and watched as two solids went in. "She checked in, but she won't tell us where she's at."

"I can find her."

Christian was tempted to take him up on the offer. He wasn't comfortable not knowing where Riley was, but she was a grown woman. She also knew how to take care of herself. "Not yet. But it may come to that."

"She's not with anyone is she?" Marshall asked right before he took his next shot.

Christian narrowed his gaze on the sheriff. "I like you, Marshall, and that's the only reason I'm giving you this one warning to stay away from my sister."

Marshall straightened, grinning, his gray eyes crinkling at the corners. "Worried she might like me?"

"Yep. Then I'd have to kill you." Christian knew how beautiful his sister was, but the

Chiasson's reputation kept the boys away from her while she still lived in Lyons Point.

Christian didn't want to think about what she had been doing while away. He closed his eyes to try and block out the mental image, but it was already there.

"You could try," Marshall said and ran a hand through his short, black hair.

Christian opened his eyes to focus on the green felt of the pool table. He looked at the balls and bent to line up his shot, but his gaze lifted to the bar and landed on Curls.

She had a drink in hand. It wasn't some frilly mixed drink, nor was it a beer. If he had to guess by the glass and color, it was bourbon. Not a drink he expected to see in Curls' hand.

Christian returned his concentration to the pool table. He lined up his cue and took his shot -- the same time Curls laughed. The sound went straight to his cock, causing him to jerk his stick just as it made contact with the ball.

He straightened as none of his balls went into the pockets. Frustrated in more ways than one, he lifted his gaze to Curls and listened to more of her laughter.

Marshall clapped him on the back and leaned in to whisper, "I'm liking your distraction."

No matter how many times Christian tried to concentrate on the game, Curls pulled his attention away time and again. Three games – and a hundred and fifty dollars later - it was obvious he was distracted.

It was after one in the morning, and if Curls hadn't been there, Christian would've already found a bed partner for the night.

But Curls was there.

"Want to go another round?" Marshall asked, laughing.

Christian cut him a dark look. "You've taken enough of my money for the night."

Marshall put away the cue sticks. "Just go talk to her."

"No."

"Why?" he asked in surprise. "You're obviously attracted to her."

Christian raised his beer to Marshall and grinned.

They moved back to the bar when others approached the table to play pool.

Marshall had a confused look on his face. "Explain something to me. You were ready to bed those two girls earlier – who left disappointed, by the way - but not this one?"

"You're on a roll tonight, Sheriff. Tell me, are you a detective or something?" Christian asked sarcastically.

It was Marshall's turn to glare. "Seriously, Christian. I don't get it."

Christian peeled the label from his beer bottle. "You know what my family does. You know the hazards we face daily."

"I do," Marshall agreed with a nod.

"It's just a matter of time before one of those monsters gets us. My brothers are the biggest kinds of dimwitted fools for bringing the women they love into this messed up life we lead."

Marshall was quiet for a moment. "Your line has to continue."

"Fortunately, it will. Between Vin, Linc, and Beau, I've no doubt there will be many little Chiassons running around soon."

"Riley, as well."

Christian shook his head. "Nope. We got her out of this life early enough so that she could lead a normal one. No doubt she'll have children, but they won't be fighting monsters like us."

"You want to be alone?"

Want had nothing to do with it. It was a matter of sanity. Christian knew that if the right kind of woman came along, he would fall in love with her.

He also knew that if he ever did fall in love and lost her, it would kill him. He wasn't just saving some unknown woman from a worry-filled life, he was preserving himself, as well.

"In a house with six people? How the hell can I ever be alone?" Christian joked.

But Marshall didn't smile. "It's no way to live."

Christian let his fake grin fade. "It's the only way I'm going to."

"Do your brothers know?"

"Yeah. They aren't happy about it, but they've come to terms with it."

Marshall finished his beer and pushed the empty bottle away. "That's messed up on so many levels. I'm outta here. I'll see you soon."

"I'm sure you will."

Marshall slid off the stool. "If I'm going to live here, I need to know everything. What better way than hangin' with the Chiassons?"

Christian waved as Marshall walked off. Once the sheriff was gone, his gaze returned to Curls. She was finishing her drink, and he watched as she paid and leaned over the bar to hug her friend. Then she was gone, too.

It was everything Christian could do not to go after her. He was going to make damn sure he never came back to Joel's Place again. Not when there was a chance Curls could be there.

Christian remained for another fifteen minutes and finished his beer. He declined an offer from a leggy blond and decided to head home.

He walked out of the bar and barely made it halfway to his truck before he caught sight of pale brown curls in the moonlight.

CHAPTER TWO

"Really?" Ivy Pierce said as she stared at her flat tire.

She had known stopping at the bar for a drink after work was a bad idea, but Stacy wouldn't accept no for an answer. It wasn't that she didn't have a good time when she was with Stacy, but her friend was usually trying to set her up with some guy.

At least this time Stacy was content to just talk. Ivy shook her head at the tire. The only thing that had gone right the entire week had been her visit with Stacy.

Lately, if something could go wrong, it did. Often. This was her second flat in three days. From her air conditioning going out, to breaking her grandmother's dish, to losing her favorite earrings...

She opened her trunk and went to get the jack when she remembered her other tire was still being repaired, which meant the spare was already in use.

"Just great," she mumbled.

She was going to have to wait for Stacy to get off work to give her a ride home. Ivy was turning to go back into the bar when dogs began barking behind her. She jumped, whirling around because it had sounded like they were racing toward her.

"Is there a problem?" asked a deep, incredibly sexy voice behind her.

Startled for the second time, Ivy turned, her hand on her throat. The man was tall and muscular, his shirt stretched tightly across his chest and arms. But his face was in shadow. She took a step back.

"Forgive me," he said and shifted so the light on the side of the building shown on his face. "Is everything all right?"

Ivy stared at him a full minute, taking in his short, dark hair and startlingly handsome face. If you liked the rugged look—which she just discovered she very much did—he was just about perfect.

She swallowed, recalling that he had asked her two questions. "I've got a flat."

"I can fix it if you'd like," he offered.

Ivy blew out a frustrated breath. "I fixed the first flat two days ago, so, unfortunately, the spare is already in use."

"I see." He looked around, a frown forming when the dogs started barking again. "Two flats so soon? You run over glass or something?"

"No. It's just been the week from hell. Everything is going wrong."

"I'm Christian, by the way."

She smiled, unable to stop herself. "I'm Ivy."

"Well, Ivy, you're in a jam. Why don't I call a tow truck for you?"

"No," she said hastily. Too hastily, if his confused look was any indication. She licked her lips. "I'll be fine."

"Out here by yourself?"

"I've got a friend coming to help," she lied.

He nodded, looking off in the distance when the barking began again – closer this time. "That's good. When are they coming?"

"In a bit."

"That's not going to be soon enough, Ivy."

His response shocked her and she took another step away from him. She heard a dog snarl behind her, but when she turned around, nothing was there.

Suddenly, she was yanked against a wall of muscle and turned so that she was pinned between Christian and her car. She could hear the growls and barking of the dogs, but she still couldn't see them.

Christian threw something that looked like dirt in the air, and the night went deathly quiet.

"Okay, Ivy, here's the deal. We're going to run to my truck. It's the gray one parked three away from yours. Get in on the driver's side and scoot over. We're not going to have a lot of time."

"I don't understand."

"I'll explain later," he said in a rush. "Now, run!"

Ivy secured her purse on her shoulder then scooted away and turned to run. She cut the corner of her car too quickly and jammed her knee into the bumper. Her foot slipped, but she managed to catch herself before she fell.

She heard Christian behind her, as well as the jingle of keys. The lights of a dark gray truck flickered as he unlocked the vehicle. She ran as fast as she could to the door and jerked it open.

"Get in!" Christian bellowed as she struggled to climb in and get into the passenger seat.

She fell forward, slamming her face into the passenger door when Christian jumped into the truck and shut them inside. Ivy sat up, trying to calm her breathing and her heart.

Something rammed into her side of the truck. She jerked her head to the window and saw something so close its breath was fogging up the glass, but she could only see the fog, not what was causing it.

Christian fired up the engine and quickly drove away. Ivy's hands were shaking as she attempted to put on her seatbelt. It took her several tries before she was finally able to get it buckled.

She stared straight ahead, her heart hammering in her chest so hard she expected it to burst at any moment.

"Are you all right?" Christian asked as he sped down the roads. "Are you bit? Scratched?"

"N...no," she stammered.

"I didn't figure you for one to make a deal."

She blinked and slowly turned her head to him. "Excuse me?"

"A deal. With a Crossroads demon."

"What are you talking about? What the hell's a Crossroads demon?"

Christian glanced at her, his blank expression illuminated by the faint glow from the truck's dashboard lights. "You don't have to lie to me. I'm a Chiasson."

"And I'm a Pierce. What has that got to do with anything?"

The night was turning more and more confusing by the minute. Ivy just wanted to be in her favorite PJs, sitting on the couch, catching up on episodes of Game of Thrones.

"I want to go home. Pull over, please."

Christian shook his head as he sped up. "I can't do that. As soon as I pull over, those Hell Hounds will be back. I doubt you'll get away a second time."

Hell Hounds? Crossroads demons? Was this some kind of sick joke?

Ivy quietly unzipped her purse and wrapped her hand around the butt of her gun. "Pull over."

"There's only one place that's safe for you. As soon as we get there, I'll explain everything."

"You'll stop now." To make him see that she was serious, Ivy drew her weapon.

Christian glanced at her, then did a double-take when he saw the gun. His lips flattened into a line as he began to slow the truck.

Ivy knew the times she'd gone to the gun range would pay off. In the cruel, vicious world, it was inevitable that someone, somewhere would try to take advantage of her. But she was prepared.

Tires squealed as Christian jerked the wheel, turning it to the right and tossing her against the center console. She screamed in outrage – and surprise.

Then she heard the dogs barking again.

Christian drove like a bat out of hell down the dirt road. The night was too dark to see anything other than what the headlights showed, which was nothing but grass on either side of them.

"Hold on. This isn't going to be pretty or smooth," Christian said tightly as he jerked the wheel once more.

The first bump jarred Ivy so much that she nearly lost her hold on the gun. She quickly shoved the weapon back in her purse and grabbed hold of anything she could to keep from hitting the top of the truck as they bounced along.

"You left the road!" she hollered.

Christian was entirely focused on the path in front of them. "Had to," was all he said.

Ivy opened her mouth to warn him of the huge hole, right before the passenger side tire went in. Her teeth clashed and her jaw slammed shut with the force of the hit. The truck lurched, causing her head to ram up against the window.

"Oww," she mumbled.

There was no more barking, but Christian

didn't slow. He drove like he was on a racetrack and their lives depended upon winning the race.

All Ivy knew was that she felt a measure of relief now that the barking had stopped. She spotted a row of crepe myrtles lining a lane as Christian swerved into the driveway.

When a large, white plantation house came into view, Ivy assumed he would slow. Instead, he sped up. Words lodged in her throat when she saw the front door of the house open and a man and woman step out.

Christian slammed on the brakes, jerking the wheel once more so that the passenger side of the truck slid toward the porch.

"Get out!" Christian ordered.

The truck door was thrown open by a man who grabbed her arm and yanked her out. She was unceremoniously tossed onto the porch where a woman with beautiful, long blond hair helped steady her.

"Are you all right?" the woman asked.

Before Ivy could answer, the barking started again.

"Shit," Christian said as he jumped from the truck onto the porch.

The man looked from Christian to Ivy. "What the hell is going on?"

"She claims to know nothing," Christian told the man.

Ivy had had enough. She stepped away from the three of them and reached her hand into her purse again. "I don't know what is wrong with all of y'all, but I'm done being scared. I'm through with being tossed about like a bag of potatoes. I'm leaving."

"If you do, you die," Christian said calmly. He faced her and held up his hands. "We can help, Ivy."

The man glowered at Christian. "The hell we can. She knew what she was getting into."

"I don't think she did."

The porch light came on, and Ivy got her first good look at the other man. He looked so similar to Christian that it was obvious they were brothers. They had the same coal black hair, the same build, and the same angry looks that they were throwing at each other.

"Hold up, Beau," the blond woman said. "Listen to Christian first." She turned to Ivy. "My name is Davena."

The front door opened again, followed by the screen door. A woman with long, black hair poked her head out. She looked at each of them and walked out onto the porch.

Christian turned to talk to his brother. "If she knew, wouldn't she have run?"

"That's what they all do," Beau said.

"She didn't," Christian said and threw a thumb over his shoulder toward Ivy. "She had no idea what they were."

Ivy felt as if her life were unraveling. "She is right here, and has no idea what y'all are talking about. Look, I'm not asking for anyone's help."

"But I think you need it," Davena said.

Christian glanced at her. "I believe her, Beau."

"There's only one way the Hell Hounds would come for her," Beau said. "She made a deal, and now it's time to pay up. With her soul."

Ivy choked. Soul. Did he just say soul? First Crossroads demons, then Hell Hounds, and now payment with her soul. Had she stepped into the Twilight Zone?

Christian walked to her and gently grabbed her shoulders. He looked down at her with eyes so bright, so vivid a blue she became lost in them. "Ivy, did you make a deal for your soul with a Crossroads demon for wealth, health, or...anything? A contract where you got what you asked for for a certain amount of time with the knowledge that you would pay with your soul when the time came?"

"A Cross... A deal..." She couldn't even finish the sentence. "No, never."

Christian's smile was soft, his gaze intense. "Your choice then. You can leave, or you can stay here and let me help you."

As if Ivy had a choice.

CHAPTER THREE

Christian glanced out at the darkness before he turned Ivy toward the house. "Let's get you inside so we can explain."

He had never been so happy to have Davena and Olivia there. If the women hadn't shown up, Christian was sure Ivy would've refused his offer.

Beau stopped Christian before he could follow the women inside. "Are you sure about this? Tangling with Hell Hounds isn't something I'm crazy about on a good day, but we've got our women here now."

"And Ivy isn't important?" Christian wasn't sure why anger filled him so rapidly, but once there, he couldn't shove it aside. "I thought it was our job to protect the innocent."

"It is. If they are innocent."

"Ivy is."

"You just met her," Beau argued.

Christian crossed his arms over his chest. "Need I remind you of how you met Davena? Or how about how Lincoln and Ava met? Better yet, what about Vincent and Olivia?"

"I get your point," Beau said tightly.

"No, you don't. I get that you have someone to protect now, but we've always had someone to protect. We had each other, and we had the innocents of this parish."

Beau ran a hand through his black hair. "It's different with a woman you love, Christian. I'd die for Davena."

"We could argue this point all night, but I'm not going to. I'm going to get to the bottom of this thing with Ivy."

"And if she's lying? What if she did make a deal? Will you really shove her off this porch and let the Hounds have her?"

That wasn't something Christian was ready to think about yet. "We protect the innocent. If she made the deal without knowing it, she's still an innocent."

"There's no getting away from a Hell Hound," Beau stated. "This house may be warded, but they'll find their way in eventually."

"I brought Ivy here. I'll be the one to protect her."

Beau turned and walked into the house without another word.

Christian blew out a deep breath. He looked

into the darkness again. The Hell Hounds were out there, waiting. They weren't regular dogs. They were invisible to humans and very intelligent. And they had one mission — to take the soul of whoever signed the deal with the demon.

Christian turned on his heel and strode into the house. As he figured, the girls had taken Ivy into Vincent's office. He stopped at the doorway and stood next to Beau. Olivia sat in a chair, while Davana took one side of the sofa. Ivy sat on the edge of the couch on the left side. She kept one hand in her purse.

Christian bit back a smile, as he knew her hand was wrapped around her gun. The woman had gumption. He applauded her for that. It was too bad the weapon couldn't help her against the Hell Hounds.

But it could do major damage to the people in this room.

He cleared his throat to get Ivy's attention. As soon as he did, the idle chitchat between Olivia and Davena ended. All eyes turned to him.

Christian walked farther into the office to rest one hip on Vincent's desk. "I'm sure you've got questions, and we'll be happy to answer them."

"But you've got questions for me first, right?" Ivy said in a remarkably calm voice.

That surprised Christian since he knew she was anything but composed by her rapid breathing and the way she kept fisting her left hand.

Her gaze met his straight on, and he was taken aback by the shade of her eyes — a beautiful mix of green and gold. Christian had never taken much interest in a woman's eye color before.

Until that moment.

Ivy shrugged but didn't remove her right hand from her purse. "Fine. Ask your questions. I'm pretty sure I answered them outside, but I'll be happy to repeat my answer – no."

Christian couldn't hide his smile. "You've got courage and a tough spirit. That just might get you through this."

Davena snorted. "Might? Christian, really. It will get her through this."

"Davena's right," Olivia told Ivy.

Ivy glanced at both women before turning her gaze back to Christian. "Where am I?"

Christian frowned. He had been so caught up in getting her to the house, and then inside, that he hadn't stopped to fill her in. "As I told you, I'm Christian Chiasson. This is my brother, Beau. The spirited one on the couch is his woman, Davena." Christian winked at Davena before he shot Olivia a grin. "The sassy one over there is Olivia, and she's engaged to my eldest brother, Vincent. As to where you are, you're at our family home."

"That's apparently someplace the things after me can't get into?" Ivy asked saucily.

Davena laughed. "Oh, I like you. You're going to fit right in. These Chiasson boys have a habit of thinking they can make all the decisions."

"Now, Davena," Beau started.

Davena held up a hand and shook her head. "Stay over there, because if you get close, you'll kiss me, and then we won't be able to stop."

"What's wrong with that?" Beau asked with a cocky grin.

Christian watched Ivy as she observed their exchange, looking as if she were confused by it. Finally. He wasn't the only one who didn't understand this thing his brothers had with their women.

"I think I should start off by telling you that the things that go bump in the night are real," Christian said to get the topic back on track.

Ivy swallowed hard. "Meaning?"

"There are ghosts, vampires, werewolves, demons, and Hell Hounds. Among other creatures. Other monsters."

Her gaze held his for a long moment. "You're not joking."

Christian shook his head. "You heard the Hounds tonight. You knew they were there, even if you couldn't see them. There's your proof."

"How do all of you," Ivy said, motioning to everyone with her hand, "know all of this?"

It was Beau who said, "Because we hunt them."

"Hunt?" Ivy repeated slowly. Her gaze moved from Beau to Christian. "You can kill ghosts and such?"

Christian nodded. "Just about every creature has a weakness, a way to be killed." He wasn't ready to tell her the Hell Hounds were the exception.

Ivy pulled her hand out of her purse and dropped her face into her palms. "This has to be a nightmare."

"I wish it was," Olivia said in a soft voice. "The sooner you face the reality of it, the sooner we can all figure out what's going on."

Davena tucked her legs to her side. "Would it help to tell you I'm a witch?"

Ivy's head snapped up to look at Davena. "A witch? Um...I'm not sure if that helps or not."

"Try to remember that we're here to help," Davena said.

Christian was going to have to remember to pull both Davena and Olivia aside to thank them later.

Beau leaned against the doorway and folded his arms across his chest. "Our family came to Lyons Point generations ago to battle the supernatural that are drawn to this area. My brothers and I carry on that tradition."

"All right," Ivy said with a nod. "I can't deny the sound I heard, or the fact that I couldn't see what was attacking the truck, even if it was obvious something was. If you do battle the supernatural, then tell me what a Crossroads demon is."

Christian shifted so that he leaned back against the desk with his hands on either side of his hips. "There are demons who can be summoned at a crossroads to make a deal, an exchange of something a person wants for their soul."

"I didn't do that," Ivy said confidently.

"Occasionally, a Crossroads demon will pick a place and set up at a bar for a week or two, looking for those who are willing to trade their souls for advancements in their careers, money, or to save someone else."

Ivy lifted her chin. "Not me either."

"It wouldn't have been recently," Beau pointed out.

Christian studied Ivy. "Normally, the amount of time given by the demon before they claim your soul is ten years. There have been instances where the demon does five or less, but the norm is ten."

"Still not me," Ivy said with a grin. "Ten years ago I was fourteen and more focused on other things. I wouldn't have even thought of trading my soul."

Beau pushed away from the doorway, dropping his hands as he walked into the room to stand before the fireplace. "Ivy, the only way a Hell Hound knows where to go is because a person is marked when they sell their soul. The Hell Hounds don't make mistakes."

"Well, they did this time," she stated. "My soul is mine."

Christian exchanged a look with Beau. "If she's telling the truth, then there has to be another reason the Hounds are after her."

"I've never read anything in Dad's journal about such an instance," Beau said.

Christian looked at the clock as he realized Vincent, Lincoln, and Ava weren't there. "Where are the others?"

"Lincoln and Ava took the west," Davena said.

Olivia pushed her hair back from her face. "Vincent went north. He said he'd be back around two or three."

That meant Beau had taken the south, which was easy to search quickly and return to the house. It could be hours before Lincoln and Ava returned. Christian wanted to talk to everyone before he said more to Ivy.

"It's been a long night," Christian said. "Why don't we all get some rest? We can talk more in the morning."

To his surprise, Ivy didn't argue. She rose with Davena and Olivia. As she followed the women out, her gaze met his.

Christian had the uncontrollable urge to touch her, to let her know that everything was going to be all right. He hated when innocents were caught in the middle of the madness involving the monsters they hunted.

That's all it was. He was angry that Ivy had been targeted. It had nothing to do with the raw, primal desire that burned through him, demanding that he learn her taste and every inch of her skin.

Once the women were gone, Christian walked around the desk. He sat in the chair and opened a lower drawer to pull out the journal their family had begun keeping from the very beginning. It was a large book that had been re-bound many times with new entries and pictures.

"If there's an explanation, it'll be in there," Beau said as he came to stand next to Christian.

"I know. My worry is if there's nothing."

"Then that means Ivy is lying."

Christian slammed his hand on the desk. "What

if she's not? Why do you have to be so goddamn quick to condemn her?"

"Why are you defending her so strongly?" Beau asked, his gaze narrowed.

Christian shook his head and went back to looking at the journal. "I already explained that."

"Right. She's an innocent. You believe her."

"And you don't," Christian answered.

The back door opened as footsteps sounded through the house. Christian looked up as Lincoln and Ava slid to a stop in the foyer when they saw them in the office. A few steps behind the couple was Vincent.

Vincent glanced from the open journal to Christian and Beau. "Why did I hear a Hell Hound close to the house?"

"Because Christian brought a woman here that the beasts want to claim," Beau answered.

Christian leaned back in the chair when four sets of eyes trained on him. He was used to having everyone looking at him for various reasons. Normally, he shrugged it off, but he knew in his gut that Ivy was innocent.

It was time he took a stand. Who better to do that for than an innocent?

A beautiful innocent with stunning hazel eyes.

CHAPTER FOUR

"There's nothing," Linc said as he slammed another book closed and shoved it across the glossy wood slats. He shifted in his spot on the floor and leaned his head back onto the cushions of the sofa.

Christian rubbed his tired eyes. "With all the books we have in this house, there has to be something."

"Nothing," Ava said from her spot on the couch. She ran her hands through Lincoln's long hair while she looked on her laptop. "Not a single thing. Isn't that odd?"

Vincent sighed heavily from the chair near the fireplace. "Very. Either it really doesn't happen, or it's so rare that no one has bothered to mention it."

"That I don't believe," Beau said. "If it

happened, then someone, somewhere would have made a record of it."

Davena made a face before she stretched her arms over her head. "I agree with Beau."

"I believe Ivy," Olivia said, smothering a yawn.

Vincent grinned at Olivia. "She might be a very good liar."

Christian squeezed his eyes closed for a moment. "There's an explanation for this. We just need to find it."

"Then we start with Ivy," Ava said.

Olivia's face was grim as she gave a nod. "A background check."

Christian didn't argue because he knew it was the only way. It didn't mean he liked it, however. While Ava and Olivia began to search the Internet for anything about Ivy Pierce, Christian kept looking through the journal.

At least the family was willing to help. Beau was the only one who had voiced his concern with the Hounds being so near his woman, but Christian had seen the worry on Vin's and Linc's faces, as well.

The only ones who seemed unperturbed by it were Olivia, Ava, and Davena. They'd each come to the Chiasson house while being pursued by the supernatural. Maybe that's why they understood.

Thirty-five minutes later, Christian glanced at the clock on the wall to see that it was almost five in the morning. No one had gotten any sleep, and Ivy would be awake soon.

"Well," Ava said. "I think I might have found

something."

Christian set aside the journal. "What is it?"

"When Ivy was three there was an accident in the bayou involving her father and her seven-year-old brother."

"Ah, damn," Lincoln murmured.

Ava looked up from the screen. "Both were killed."

"That left Ivy and her mother," Olivia said.

Ava lowered her gaze to the computer again. "Yep. Their life was relatively quiet until five years later when Ivy got sick. Very sick."

Christian's gut clenched at the news.

"She was in and out of the hospital for the next six years. The doctors couldn't figure out what was wrong with her. Several times, she nearly died."

Vincent ran a hand across his jaw. "Is she still sick?"

"No," Davena said. "She's healthy as a horse."

"Then what cured her?" Beau asked.

Ava shrugged. "It doesn't say. The medical records just stop."

Olivia nodded. "Ava's right. The next thing that shows up in any public record is Ivy on the debate team in high school."

Now Christian knew where she got her argumentative talents. He looked over to see Davena mumbling with her eyes closed. She was doing a spell, but he didn't know what for. Before he had a chance to ask, Beau was talking.

"We need to know what was wrong with Ivy all those years, as well as how she was cured," Beau said.

Christian sat back in the chair and glared at his brother. "You think she made a deal with a demon to get better."

"She was a kid!" Beau shouted. "She was dying. Yes, I think a demon might have found her and offered her a way out."

"Don't you think she would've remembered that?" Vincent asked.

Beau shrugged. "You'd think."

"Perhaps she hasn't put two and two together," Lincoln offered.

Christian shoved the chair away from the desk so hard it rolled back against the wall behind him. He stood and walked out of the room.

He didn't understand why everyone was assuming that Ivy was lying. Why couldn't they see that she might very well be telling the truth?

His name was called, but he was done with the family for the moment. He needed some time alone, some time to collect his thoughts and go over everything that had happened.

Christian walked into his room, closing the door behind him. He fell face first on the bed before he turned his head to the side and closed his eyes.

All he saw was light brown curls and hazel eyes. He heard Ivy's laughter, felt her fear. He had looked into her clear eyes on the porch and accepted her answer as truth.

Was he wrong? He hadn't been before. Then again, he hadn't felt such desire for a woman either.

Though that wasn't what was driving him.

It was the unshakable knowledge that he had to help Ivy. He hadn't told his brothers that, nor would he. It wasn't that he was afraid to tell them. It was because they would think he was interested in her.

Boy was he interested, but only for a night of rousing sex. Other than that, there was nothing.

A flash of her face lined with fear as she pointed her gun at him filled his mind.

She was a handful. She didn't hide her panic, instead, she worked through it. Showed strength in spite of it. What else could she do after losing her father and brother at such a young age? She probably didn't remember them, but she certainly remembered all the hospital visits. That alone explained so much about her.

Christian cleared his mind and let sleep claim him.

~ ~ ~

Ivy showered and put her clothes from the previous day back on before she stepped out of the bedroom she had been given for the night. Oddly enough, she had slept like the dead once she'd fallen asleep.

The house was quiet, but a delicious smell was wafting up from the kitchen. She made her way down the stairs and followed her nose to the source.

She saw Beau with his chin-length black hair

cooking. He had his back to her, so she took a step back to leave when she ran into someone.

Startled, Ivy whirled around to find another man with the same intense blue eyes and black hair as Christian and Beau.

The man smiled, his long black hair hanging loose to his shoulders. "No need to leave. Beau makes the best waffles around."

Ivy opened her mouth, trying to come up with an excuse to leave when the man gently took her arm and led her to a chair at the rectangular table in the kitchen.

"I'm Lincoln, by the way. Second eldest. Ava is still asleep. She needs at least eight hours or she is in full-on grouch mode," he said with a smile.

"Ivy Pierce," she said with a nod.

Lincoln sat across from her and folded his hands on the table. "Christian filled us in when we got home last night."

"Do you think I'm lying as Beau does?" she said. No sense in tiptoeing around it.

Beau didn't so much as twitch at her comment.

Lincoln glanced at Beau, his smile widening. "If you'd come a few months ago, I suspect things would have been different. It wasn't until recently that we expanded our family. Until then, it was a house of bachelors. Then Olivia returned to Lyons Point when something was killing any woman a Chiasson so much as showed interest in. Vincent had been in love with Olivia since school, and that put her in danger."

Ivy sat back, interested in the tale.

Lincoln shrugged and reclined in the chair. "We found the culprits and killed them. Although by that time, Vin knew he couldn't let Olivia go. Then my Ava came to town. She knew Olivia, but she also had her own history here."

"Anything after her?"

Lincoln's smile slipped. "A Voodoo priestess who had – has – a grudge against Ava's father sent our cousin here to kill her."

Ivy was mortified. "What?"

"Spells were used on Kane. He couldn't stop what Delphine had done to him." Lincoln suddenly grinned. "But we saved the day, and I got my Ava."

Ivy glanced at Beau. She jerked her head to him while looking at Lincoln.

"Beau's woman, Davena, is from New Orleans. Her mother was a witch, as was her sister, though neither had even a portion of the magic within Davena. They were both killed. Davena's mother quite some time ago, and Davena's sister, Delia, more recently when Delphine, the Voodoo priestess who tried to kill Ava, came here for Davena. Beau wouldn't let that happen. Together, he and Davena won."

"So, Delphine is dead?" Ivy asked.

Beau snorted loudly. "If only."

Lincoln caught her gaze. "The point is, Ivy, we're not a house of bachelors anymore."

"You each have someone you love. Someone besides family." She nodded in understanding. "As long as I'm here, the Hell Hounds will be, as well. You're worried."

Lincoln lifted one shoulder. "There is always something after us, but Hell Hounds can't be seen. They're invisible."

So that's why she hadn't been able to see them!

"I didn't sell my soul," Ivy repeated.

Lincoln leaned forward and covered her hand with one of his. "I never said you did. I just wanted to explain why some might be acting a certain way."

Ivy couldn't exactly fault Beau for wanting to protect Davena. "I understand."

"Now," Lincoln said as he once more reclined. "Let's catch you up on us. Vin is the eldest, and I'm next in line. After that is Christian, then Beau. Bringing up the rear of the Chiasson children is Riley, our only sister. Fortunately, she's not here to be in the middle of all of this."

Ivy was raised as an only child. The concept of siblings was as foreign to her as the supernatural.

She listened as Lincoln went on to talk of the house and all the wards that would keep her protected. Davena was going to extend the wards to cover the back yard, in order to give them all some room to walk.

Ivy was about to thank Lincoln when her neck heated. She touched her hand to it before she turned her head to find Christian in the doorway staring at her.

Their gazes met, held. He was freshly showered, his hair still damp. And he looked too damn gorgeous for his own good.

If she thought his eyes were vivid the night

before, in the light of day, they were so bright she couldn't look away.

"Did you sleep well?" Christian asked as he walked into the kitchen and over to the coffee pot on the counter.

"Yes." Why was her voice so breathless? "You?"

He shrugged before turning and setting a mug of coffee in front of her. "I slept."

She frowned since he'd said it as if that answered everything. Ivy wrapped her hands around the mug. She looked down into the dark liquid. "I'll understand if y'all want me to leave. You have something precious here, and it shouldn't be shattered."

There was a moment of silence. Then a chair scraped on the floor as Christian pulled it out and sat.

Ivy finally gave in and looked up. Christian was once more staring at her.

"You're not going anywhere, darlin'."

CHAPTER FIVE

Christian stared at Ivy from the kitchen window as she stood on the porch, her gaze directed toward the bayou. There was a slight chill to the morning that was quickly disappearing with the rising sun.

Beau came to stand beside him. "We need to know more about her illness."

"In other words, you want me to talk to her," Christian said.

"You brought her here."

Christian sighed because he knew Beau was right. It wasn't that he didn't want to talk to Ivy. No, it was that he did want to talk to her. That alone had kept him from going to her all morning.

"You look at her as if you don't know what to do with her," Beau said with a snort. "We all know you've never had a problem with women."

Christian watched as Ivy let out a deep breath, her shoulders sagging. Beau was talking again, but Christian wasn't paying attention.

He pushed away from the window, walked around Beau and exited the house. Christian didn't like the way Ivy tensed when she heard the door.

"Would you rather be alone?"

She shook her head. "I've been expecting someone to want to talk more. It's just that I don't like being under a microscope with everyone watching me."

He knew that had to do with her times in the hospital. Christian walked to the other side of the porch to give her some room. He didn't want to crowd her, plus, the more distance between them, the better.

"I'm going to help you with this problem," he said.

Ivy turned her head, a slight smile pulling at her lips. "I believe you're going to try. I did my own research this morning on Hell Hounds. There is no helping me."

The sunlight bathed her in a red-orange light that turned her hair auburn. For an instant, she looked otherworldly, as if she didn't belong on Earth.

Then she ducked her head before returning her gaze to the bayou. The sun continued its ascent, and the moment was lost.

But Christian would forever hold the memory.

He swallowed and remembered why he was out there with her. "Demons aren't just vicious and cruel. They're also cunning and crafty. They're calculating, and if they see an opportunity, they'll do whatever they need to in order to get what they want."

"You think I was tricked?"

"It's a possibility. I need details, Ivy."

"About my life?"

He couldn't take his eyes from her. Christian leaned a shoulder against one of the porch's columns and crossed his arms over his chest. "Yes."

"There's not much to tell." She faced him then. "My father and brother died in an accident out in the bayou when I was three. It was just my mother and me until last year. She had a heart attack."

"I'm sorry." Life certainly hadn't been kind to her, but then again, fate had a way of knowing who could handle such things. Ivy was a strong person. It was evident in everything about her.

Ivy shrugged. "It happens."

"Yes, it does. My parents were killed when I was just a boy. They died on the same night."

Their eyes locked. Her gaze wasn't filled with pity. It was filled with understanding, as only someone who had experienced such things could have.

"It's been just us five for a long time," Christian continued.

"At least y'all had each other."

"Yeah. My brothers are a pain in the ass, but I wouldn't have survived that night without them. We needed to be strong for Riley, too. She was so young. She didn't really comprehend it all at first."

"She's very lucky to have you."

Christian wasn't so sure his sister felt that way, not after the latest fiasco. How could they have been so wrapped up in things that they hadn't realized she had graduated from the University of Texas?

"She came home recently. We had just defeated Delphine for a second time, and we never wanted Riley involved with the family business." Christian ran a hand down his face. What was it about Ivy that made him want to spill his guts? "We didn't exactly give her a warm welcome. In fact, I'm pretty sure Vin told her to return to Austin immediately."

Ivy's forehead furrowed. "Is that where she's at?"

"We don't know where she is anymore. She called and told us she was fine, but she's still angry."

"As she should be. What were y'all thinking?" Ivy admonished. "You're her family."

If Christian didn't think he could feel any lower, all he had to do was hear Ivy use that disappointed voice and he was proven wrong. "She won't answer my calls."

"Give her time. She'll come around."

"Delphine is dangerous, Ivy. We have each other here, but we don't know where Riley is. If she's alone, she could be targeted."

Ivy raised her brows. "Then you better start leaving some heartfelt messages to get her to call you back."

"Probably." His mind was already past Riley and centered squarely on Ivy. "You've been alone for a year?"

She nodded, her gaze lowering to the porch for a moment. "I have. There are times it's bad, but the days are getting better. I work from home as a medical transcriptionist, so I can make my own schedule."

"Interesting."

She laughed, her eyes twinkling. "Now you're making fun of me."

"Never," he vowed, his smile growing.

Silence stretched as they stared at each other again. Christian was thankful he was so far away from her on the porch because if he had been closer, he would've kissed her.

"So, no one new in your life?" he asked after he cleared his throat.

She looked pointedly at him. "Just you and your family. Before that, no one."

"You're not seeing someone?" It was a valid question, though he wanted to know the answer for himself, not for the investigation.

"No."

One simple word, but with it, Christian wanted to rejoice. Then he reminded himself that he didn't care. He didn't want a relationship.

Of any kind.

"Do you want to know my favorite color, as well?" she asked with a grin.

Christian laughed as he dropped his arms and

pushed away from the column. "I'm sorry I'm prying into your life."

"It's all right. I'll tell you anything you want to know. I don't want to die."

That wiped his smile away instantly. He didn't want her to die either. "Did anything significant happen ten years ago?"

"That's right. The ten-year deal thing." Her face scrunched up as she considered his words. "I left the hospital for the last time and got better."

Christian knew of her illness, but hearing her say it was like a punch in the gut. "You were sick?"

"Yes, but no one could diagnose what was wrong with me. I was sick for years. In and out of the hospital all the time. I missed so much school that my mother decided to homeschool me."

"You look healthy."

She glanced down at herself. "Now. Back then, I could barely lift my hand from the bed. My mother had to feed me. My mind worked great, but my body...well, didn't. No one could get near me because a simple cold could kill me."

"My God." Christian didn't know what else to say.

Ivy tucked a curl behind her ear and put her hands in the back pockets of her jeans as she glanced at the bayou once more. "All the poking and prodding by the doctors, and the numerous medications I was on eventually worked. Though I fear that whatever it was will return one day."

To be miraculously healed like that wasn't something that happened often. Usually, it meant that magic or a demon was involved.

"Did anyone visit you in the hospital and ask what you would do if you weren't sick anymore?"

Ivy's head cocked to the side. "I thought of that last night, but besides my doctors and the nurses, my mother was the only one who visited."

"The demon could've been a nurse or doctor."

She was shaking her head before he finished. "None of them ever asked me such a thing."

"Then I'm out of ideas," Christian said in frustration.

As soon as the words were out of his mouth, he thought of her mother. She would have wanted Ivy to get better more than anything. The same thought must have crossed Ivy's mind because her face crumpled.

"Ivy," he said and took a step toward her.

She raised a hand to stop him and stepped back. "My mother was devout in her beliefs. She wouldn't have traded my soul in such a way."

"She couldn't." Christian rubbed the back of his neck, feeling like the biggest ass for having to say his next words. "Ivy, the only soul a person can bargain with is their own."

"You think she sold her soul?"

"It's the only thing that makes sense."

"Then why are the Hell Hounds after me?"

It was a good question. "Your mother died last year, right?"

"In her sleep. The autopsy showed it was a heart attack."

"If that's the case, then the Hell Hounds should

be satisfied. They got their soul, even if they didn't have to come to get it."

Ivy gave a little shake of her head. "That still doesn't explain why the Hounds are after me."

"It's time we found out."

Christian strode back into the house with Ivy on his heels. They walked into the office. He went to the desk and sat, once more pulling out the journal.

He glanced up and pointed to one of the laptops sitting on the coffee table. "Do you mind looking up your scenario?"

"Not at all." Ivy sat, pulling the laptop to her and opening it.

Christian thumbed through the journal until he came to the part about the Hell Hounds while he heard Ivy punching the keyboard.

"What's going on?" Vincent asked as he walked in.

Christian didn't look up from his perusal of the passages. "We think Ivy's mom might have made the deal, but she died last year of a heart attack."

"That shouldn't matter then," Vin said. "The Hounds got their soul."

"Exactly." Christian glanced up at his eldest brother. "Then why are they after Ivy?"

Vincent let out a whistle that sounded throughout the house. In a matter of moments, everyone would be in the room.

Vin walked to the bookshelf and drew out two books. "Looks like we need to alter our research."

Christian slid his gaze to Ivy to find her

watching him. He gave her a nod, and her answering grin did funny things to his insides.

He decided to chalk it up to the four waffles he'd eaten.

CHAPTER SIX

Ivy was about ready to call it a day after eight hours of research when Beau let out an expletive.

"What?" Christian asked.

She still couldn't believe how hard he was working to help her. Yet, she couldn't figure out why. He didn't know her. Sure, his family helped the innocent, but for him to go to such extremes just seemed...odd.

At least, she had never encountered anyone who would do such a thing. Granted, her experience with people was limited, but she'd watched enough TV to know it was unusual.

Beau's gaze landed on her. Ivy straightened, wondering what she had done.

"I found something," Beau said as he rose from his chair and walked to her. He handed her the book, his finger next to the third paragraph on the page. "Read that out loud, please."

Ivy took the book as she set the laptop next to her. She took a deep breath and started reading. "Hell Hounds, by all accounts, are simply animals doing the bidding of the Demon of Souls. They're not just beasts, however. Special care should be taken when trying to dodge them."

She paused, not liking what she was reading so far. "Once a person makes a deal with one of the many Crossroads demons and sells their soul, it's owned by the Demon of Souls."

"We know all of this," Lincoln said.

Beau motioned for Ivy to keep going. "Finish the passage."

Ivy shrugged and returned her gaze to the book. "A soul can't be bought back. Once sold, it is lost forever. A person normally has ten years before the Hell Hounds are sent to retrieve their soul — and take the person to Hell. For the few who trade their souls to help another, the same rules apply."

She stopped reading because the implication that her mother had sold her soul to help her made her chest feel as if it were caving in from the weight of it all.

Suddenly, Christian was sitting beside her. He met her gaze briefly before he leaned over and finished for her. "There is one known instance where a person who sold their soul to help another died before their ten years came due. The Hell Hounds were then sent to the one who was saved to retrieve their soul.

"After a lengthy investigation, it was discovered the original deal-maker killed themselves to prevent having to face the Hell Hounds."

Ivy shoved the book off her and stood. She paced before the fireplace. "No. My mother didn't kill herself. There was an autopsy. They would've found it."

"No one said your mother committed suicide," Christian said.

But everyone was thinking it. Including Ivy. She stopped and tried to draw in a calming breath. "What this tells me is that despite not having made the deal, the Hell Hounds are still coming for my soul."

"Actually, no," Christian said as he finished reading something in the book. "They can't."

Beau nodded. "He's right. You didn't sell your soul."

"Then why come after me?" Ivy was getting more confused by the minute.

Christian set the open book on the coffee table before him. "They'll kill you, taking you to Hell to show the person who did sell their soul."

"Oh. Well, that makes everything better then," she said sarcastically. Ivy put her hand on her forehead. "I'm sorry. That was uncalled for."

Ava rose and came to stand beside her. "It's very much called for."

Ivy was dipping back into feeling sorry for herself like she had done as a kid in the hospital. Things were out of her control then, and it was happening all over again.

"I think that's enough research for the night," Lincoln said as he closed the book he'd been reading. He replaced it on the bookshelf and clicked on the CD player.

Music came over the speakers. Ivy recognized a song by Hozier as one she really liked. As if it were some sort of cue, everyone put away his or her books and computers.

Ivy could only stare in confusion as the three couples came together. Lincoln and Ava began to slow dance next to her while Olivia sat on Vincent's lap behind the desk and began kissing him. Beau was smiling as Davena danced to him. His arms snaked out and caught her, pulling her against him as they began to kiss, as well.

Ivy tried not to look at Christian, but she couldn't stop herself. He had his head down, as if he could pretend nothing was happening by not looking.

She quietly made her way around Lincoln and Ava and walked out of the house. That morning, she had watched the sun rise above the trees, now she was watching it sink behind them.

Davena had told her the back property was warded, including the boathouse. Ivy stepped off the porch, waiting for a Hell Hound to take her. When nothing happened, she took another couple of steps. Then a couple more.

Finally, she walked to the door of the small structure and opened it. The cages she saw inside drew her up short. Then she realized the guys had to have somewhere to put the monsters.

Ivy spotted the huge sliding metal door and cracked it open a bit. She smiled as she finished pulling it all the way open and took in the water lapping at her feet.

She sat down and leaned against the side of the door, listening to the cicadas fill the night with their music.

A sound drew her attention to the door she'd walked through. She saw a silhouette and recognized Christian.

"Couldn't take it either, I see," he said.

She laughed. "That was...awkward."

"You're the only one who understands my need to have my own place. I'm surrounded by couples on a daily basis."

"I find it hard to believe you don't have someone."

He made a face as he drew closer. "Not me."

"Relationships are complicated. I'd rather keep things simple."

"Exactly." He leaned against the opposite side of the door.

"I like to answer only to myself." His grin made her laugh. "You're looking at me as if you're not sure whether to believe me or not."

He shrugged a shoulder. "Normally, women want to talk about how soon they can get married, and how many kids they want while explaining how they're going to change their men."

Ivy nodded since she had a couple of friends just like that. "Why do women always want to change their men?"

"Good question. I'd like the answer to that, as well."

She looked away when she couldn't handle his intense gaze any longer. He seemed to be able to see right into her mind, and she didn't want him to know how many times she thought about running her hands over his body or ripping his clothes off.

"No hunting tonight?" she asked into the silence.

The music from the house rose, drifting outside as if those inside had opened windows.

"Not with the Hell Hounds after you. We're better all together."

His voice was a seduction all its own. Ivy closed her eyes. Did he know how his voice affected her? Is that why he lowered it, making his words come out as soft as silk?

"Lincoln had the right idea. We need to take our minds off Hell Hounds," Christian said as he pushed away from the doorway.

Ivy's eyes snapped open to look at him as he sat near her. His black hair tempted her fingers to touch the strands and see if they were as soft as they looked.

"I used to come out here all the time to get away from the craziness of the house," Christian said and looked straight ahead. "I'd sit right here and listen to the sounds of the bayou, watch gators and turtles swim past, and try to pretend that my life didn't involve the supernatural."

Ivy pulled her gaze from Christian to look at the purple and pink-streaked sky. "It's beautiful here. A place of solace."

"It's that and much more."

She felt his eyes on her. Unable to stop herself, Ivy turned her head to him. She wanted Christian, and the seductive music wasn't helping matters at all.

He turned toward her and tugged on a lock of her hair. "Curls. That's what I called you when I first saw you in the bar."

She raised a brow. So, he had noticed her. Ivy would've had to be blind not to appreciate such a fine specimen herself. She had taken plenty of peeks as he had leaned over to shoot pool.

"Having been sick for so long, I have a habit of not waiting around for things." She swallowed, hoping she wasn't about to make a fool of herself. "I'd like to take my mind off the current mess. Interested?"

"As if you have to ask," he said before his hand slid into her hair and around to the back of her neck as his lips covered hers.

Ivy leaned forward, her hands going to his chest. She slowly moved them up to his shoulders and then around his neck. The kiss was fiery, passionate.

She was up on her knees with him as their bodies came together. His arms wrapped around her tightly, pulling her close, his hands roaming everywhere.

His kisses took her breath away while enflaming her already burning desire. She tugged up his shirt to feel his skin.

The kiss broke long enough for him to rip off his tee. Their gazes met as he cupped her face. She was drowning in his blue eyes, sinking into the passion that enfolded them.

Then they were kissing again. Ivy wasn't sure when her shirt was removed, and she didn't care. She was living in the moment. Life was so fragile and could be taken at any moment. She wasn't going to wait around. She was going to enjoy whatever time she had left.

What better way than in the arms of a man who made her crave his touch?

Christian lowered them until they were lying on the concrete floor. She belatedly realized that she was on his shirt.

He rose over her and leaned back on his haunches. "You have to be the most interesting person I've ever met."

"Then you must not have met very many people," she said.

He removed her boots and then slowly unbuttoned her jeans. Ivy tugged them over her hips. Then she was in nothing but her bra and panties.

"My turn," she said as she sat up and reached for the waist of his jeans. She unbuttoned them, opening them wide.

The trail of chest hair narrowed at his belly button and disappeared into his waistband. She ran her hands over his impressive chest and wide shoulders. His skin was warm, his muscles hard beneath her palms.

She had known he would have an amazing body, but she hadn't been prepared for such sheer gorgeousness. His skin was bronzed from time in the sun, and there were marks from wounds that looked like slashes from talons. There were even some healed bite marks.

"I live a hard life," he said.

She lifted her gaze to his face as she traced one of his scars. "These show how powerful and resilient you are."

In answer, he claimed her mouth in a kiss that was both savage and tender.

Their arms went around each other as they gave in to the passion.

CHAPTER SEVEN

Christian burned. With each kiss, he yearned for Ivy even more. Her skin was soft as down, her kisses as intoxicating as the finest bourbon.

He ran his hand down her side, feeling her warmth beneath his palm. She yanked down his jeans, and he quickly stepped out of them. Then he hooked his thumbs in her panties and lowered them.

With a little flick, he tossed the lace away. Her leg lifted to wrap around his hips. Christian groaned and rocked his aching cock against her.

A shiver raced along his skin as her nails lightly scoured down his back. He rolled them until he was on his back and she was straddling him.

She ended the kiss and looked at him. Christian's breath locked in his lungs as her brown curls framed her face in disarray. Her lips were swollen while her eyes burned with desire.

She was the most beautiful thing he had ever laid eyes on. Ivy didn't hide her passion, didn't shield her sexuality as some women ashamed of their bodies did. No, his Ivy held his gaze as she sat up, her fingers caressing his chest.

Then she reached behind her and unhooked her bra. The garment sagged, and she gave a little shift of her shoulders until the straps fell away. With a flick of her wrist, she tossed the garment aside.

Christian's mouth went dry as he stared at her breasts. They were full and rose-tipped. He cupped them, feeling their weight.

A smile pulled at his lips when her nipples hardened before his gaze. He lifted his eyes to find Ivy had closed hers, her lips parted and a look of bliss on her face.

Christian lightly tweaked a nipple, causing Ivy to suck in a breath and her nails to dig into his chest. He let his gaze devour her, committing every inch of her to memory.

He sat up and took a turgid peak in his mouth as he braced a hand on her back to hold her. Her breaths became ragged, her hips moving slowly back and forth.

"Christian," she murmured as her head dropped back.

Moving from one breast to the other, Christian lavished attention on her amazing assets. But he wanted – needed – more.

He needed her. To be inside her, to fill her and

have their bodies joined in a dance as old as time.

Christian was surprised when she rose up further on her knees and wrapped her hand around his aching rod. He groaned at the feel of her fingers around him, stroking up and down his length.

The pleasure was intense, deep. Ivy brought a part of him to the surface that he hadn't even known was inside him. She didn't let him hold anything back, but forced him to see what was before them – to grasp it with both hands.

Her head lifted and she caught his gaze. It was the most erotic, decadent experience of his life to be looking into her passion-filled hazel eyes as she caressed his cock.

Thoughts deserted him when she brought his rod to her entrance and slowly lowered herself. He held her close, watching the desire fill her face as he stretched her.

Ivy thought she knew passion. She thought she knew what it meant to desire a man.

That was until Christian.

He opened a whole new world to her, one where she wasn't afraid to be herself, where she didn't have to hide her wantonness. With Christian, his every look urged her to let it all loose.

In his arms, the world was spinning out of control, but it was glorious. And right. She didn't search for a way to stop it. Instead, she embraced the feeling – and Christian.

Her body tightened around him deep inside of her. It took a moment to adjust to the fullness, but oh the feeling was wondrous.

Ivy looked down into his bright blue eyes and wished she knew what he was thinking. Then she rocked her hips and it no longer mattered.

Need had been building inside. It had flamed bright with their kisses earlier, but now it engulfed her. Her veins burned with it.

She moved, slowly at first, but with increasing intensity. His large hands held her firmly as their breaths mingled. Sweat beaded on their skin and the world fell away.

She wrapped her arms around his neck, holding on tight when he gripped her hips and began to move her up and down his length.

The desire coiled tighter, bringing her closer and closer to the precipice of pleasure.

Christian's lips were on her neck, kissing and nipping at her flesh. In the next instant, she was on her back as he leaned over her, the muscles in his arms bulging as he held himself up.

She was powerless to look away from him. He held still a moment before slowly pulling out of her then thrusting deep.

Ivy moaned loudly. Her breathing quickened, and she locked her legs around his waist. His hips began to pump as he moved in and out of her, alternating from long, slow thrusts to quick, hard ones.

She was hurtling quickly toward release. He worked her body expertly, leaving her no choice but to give in to all that he demanded of her.

Christian loved the sound of Ivy's moans and cries of pleasure. They spurred him to push her –

them – further, deeper into the desire enveloping them. It alarmed him that he so eagerly sought what he had been actively avoiding.

But how could he shun what Ivy so freely gave?

How could he deny both of them what providence, chance, or destiny had put in their paths?

He felt Ivy's body begin to tighten. Her nails dug deeply into his arms. He bent and licked a nipple before lightly nipping it.

She jerked, pure ecstasy crossing her face as her body convulsed around him. Christian attempted to hold back his own orgasm, but the feel of her clutching him was too much.

He gritted his teeth until he could stand it no more. With one last thrust, he gave in to his body. The climax was powerful, taking him to a place he had never been before.

The waves of pleasure swamped them again and again, prolonging their orgasms. When Christian could finally lift his head, he looked down to find a smile on Ivy's face, her eyes closed.

"Let's stay like this for a little longer," she said, cracking open one eye.

Christian was in no hurry to shatter what they had found. He pulled out of her and rolled to the side, pulling her against him as the first drops of rain began to land on the roof of the boathouse.

~ ~ ~

Ivy was the first to wake hours later. The rain

was still coming down with the clouds hiding the moon and stars. She remained in Christian's arms for a little longer, enjoying the quiet and tranquility of the moment.

There had been no sign of the Hell Hounds, but she knew it was only a matter of time before they came for her. She had no wish to die, but she didn't like putting everyone helping her in danger either.

She didn't know how much time had passed since she'd awoken, but she gradually removed Christian's arm from her waist and got to her feet. It took her a few minutes to find her clothes and put them on.

Ivy straightened from putting on her boots to find Christian awake and propped on an elbow, watching her. For once she didn't worry about what to say. They had decided on things from the start.

"Awake already?" he asked.

Ivy smiled and patted her stomach. "In need of food, actually."

"Listen, Ivy," Christian began.

She stopped him before he could go on. "There's no need. We agreed to this. We needed each other. But no strings, no ties. No need to make up excuses. It was a one-time thing."

"That's...a first for me." He flashed a grin. "I'm never very good at the excuses anyway."

"There's no need to worry. I promise not to fall in love with you."

There was a ghost of a frown, but it was quickly

covered by his smile. "That's good then."

"Want any food?"

"No, thanks. I'm going to stay out here and listen to the rain without having to be suffocated by the couples in the house."

Ivy laughed, watching how his muscles rippled when he laid on his back and placed his hands behind his head. "See you in the morning."

"See ya."

Ivy walked out of the shed with a smile, but her expression quickly changed. It wasn't the rain soaking her that made her frown. It was the strange, unnamable feeling within her that suggested she had made a mistake brushing Christian off so suddenly.

Though she didn't know why she felt that way. Neither of them wanted any kind of relationship.

Right?

Ivy reached the porch and shook off as much of the rain as she could. She removed her boots before she walked into the house. The blast of cold air from the air conditioning gave her a chill.

A glance around the kitchen uncovered a dishtowel by the sink that she used to wipe the rain from her face and arms. It was while she was putting the towel back that she realized she wasn't alone.

Ivy turned her head and met Beau's blue eyes. He was at the table with a tall glass of milk and a stack of cookies.

"There's food in the fridge," he said.

She nodded, feeling as if she were a teenager

getting caught sneaking back into the house. "Thanks."

"I should warn you that Christian likes women. He enjoys their company and their bodies, but he isn't the kind of guy who will give you a future."

Ivy's hackles immediately went up, even though she told herself it was just a brother looking out for his family. "No need to worry. I don't have designs on Christian. He's a good guy, but that's where things stop."

Beau frowned, his head cocking to the side. "Really?"

"Really." She laughed then and turned to open the fridge. She peered inside and found the foil-covered plates. She took one out and set it on the counter. "Even if the Hell Hounds weren't after me, my life is hectic enough without adding a relationship to the mix."

She took off the foil and looked at the large portion of etouffee spooned over rice. Ivy popped the plate in the microwave and heated it, feeling Beau's eyes still on her.

"Why?" Beau asked.

The microwave beeped. Ivy opened the door and stirred the food with a fork before testing the temperature. She removed the plate and set it on the table, then poured a glass of sweet tea and sat across from Beau.

"My health. If my mother did sell her soul to make me better, who's to say the illness won't return?" She shrugged and took a small bite. "My mother's life came to a halt when she needed to take care of me. I won't put someone else through that."

"And if you never get sick again?"

Ivy gave him a rueful smile. "Let's be honest here. We both know I'm not going to get away from the Hell Hounds. I have one more day. Maybe."

His frown increased as he sat forward, putting his forearms on the table. "You're going to give up so easily?"

"I don't want to die," she stated. "I'm just trying to be realistic. In all the research each of you have so graciously done, no one has found a way for me to get away from the Hounds."

Ivy took a bite of food and stared at her plate as she chewed. She didn't want to give up. But she knew what she had read. There was no getting out of this. She figured Beau would be rejoicing since she would be gone.

Beau picked up his milk and cookies and stood. "We'll find a way, Ivy. Christian risked his life to help you. The least you can do is give him some time."

CHAPTER EIGHT

Christian didn't sleep after Ivy left. He watched the rain the rest of the night until it finally tapered off and the sun rose.

Only then did he gather his clothes and dress. His thoughts had been on Ivy the entire time. He had been happy, and then confused by her quick dismissal of their lovemaking.

Though he was puzzled about why that made him angry. He should be ecstatic. He didn't have to lie to get away from a woman for once.

He should be clicking his heels in joy. Instead, he felt...sad.

He knew he had been made to taste Ivy's kiss, to know her body. They were meant to come together and know each other so carnally.

Christian's arms missed holding her against

him. Her arms hadn't just held him in return. She had shattered him then put him back together with a simple touch.

He stood in the doorway to the boathouse and looked out at the bayou. For once it wasn't him pushing a woman away. It was Ivy doing the pushing. He wanted to be closer.

How the hell had that happened? When had it happened?

Christian ran a hand down his face and sighed wearily. He knew how to woo women to his bed. He was a master at rejecting them. What he didn't know how to do was win one over.

He fished out his cell from his pocket and scrolled through his favorites. He dialed a number and put the phone to his ear.

It rang four times before a sleepy voice came from the other end. "Hello?"

"Riley?"

There was a beat of silence, then his sister said, "It's early, Christian."

"I know. I'm sorry to wake you. Are you doing okay?"

"Yeah."

He closed his eyes briefly. "That's good."

"What up?" she asked, her voice coming through clearer as she woke. "You sound troubled."

"Just the usual. Thanks for finally answering my call. I've left you several messages."

"I got them."

He nodded, then remembered she couldn't see

him. "Good, good. I'm sorry, Riley. We didn't do it right, but please understand that we were just trying to protect you."

She sighed loudly. "I'm a Chiasson, you big idiot. There's no running from what is part of my DNA."

"You deserve a normal life."

"Did it ever occur to you morons that I would rather be with my family facing the supernatural every day, than having what you consider a normal life?" she asked, her voice deepening in anger.

Christian felt like a heel. None of them had bothered to ask Riley what she wanted. "No, sis. We didn't."

"I know what y'all did was out of love," she said in exasperation. "I went away because it's what each of you were pushing for. Only I foolishly thought I'd be able to return home afterward."

"I don't want to make you angry. I didn't call to hash out what we did wrong."

"Then why did you call?" she demanded.

Christian leaned back against the doorway. "I just wanted to hear your voice."

"Bullshit. I know you, Christian. I know that tone. Something's happened. What is it?" she urged.

"I...well, I've been given the brushoff from a woman." He frowned when he heard a bubble of laughter drift over the phone before Riley smothered it.

"Wow. I never thought I'd hear you say that."

Christian rubbed his forehead. "Look, I don't

know what I'm feeling right now. It's all confusing."

"Answer me this. Do you want to see her again?"

"Yes."

Riley whistled. "You've got it bad. You never sleep with the same woman twice."

Christian prayed for patience as Riley spoke. He hadn't intended to talk to her about Ivy, but it just all came out before he could stop it.

"If you want to see her again, then make it happen," Riley said.

"I don't know how."

She laughed. "Oh, but you do, Christian. You're charming. Win her over. She'll never be able to withstand you."

"What if she does?"

"Then she's not worth your time. Though, I'd love to meet the woman who made my brother reconsider everything just to spend more time with her."

Christian couldn't help but smile as he thought of Ivy. "Her name is Ivy. She's confident, brave, and beautiful."

"She sounds perfect for you," Riley said with a smile in her voice.

He released a breath. "Come home, Riley. Please."

"Soon," she said and ended the call.

Christian pocketed the phone and leaned his head back against the doorway. He did want to see Ivy again, and not just to make love to her.

After so many years of knowing he would never settle down, it felt odd to crave someone so much. If he let Ivy into his life, she could die.

"Who am I kidding?" he asked himself. "She's already in danger with the Hell Hounds after her."

He hadn't wanted to care about a woman and be put in such a position where he worried about keeping her safe. Yet, somehow, he ended up doing exactly that.

"Stupid fate," he grumbled.

He was perfectly fine before Ivy.

Liar. You were empty, hollow. There was a void inside you that you refused to acknowledge.

Christian squeezed his eyes closed. He had been all of those things and more, but it had been worth it not to feel for someone so deeply. Then along came Curls. With her confidence and pluck. He hadn't stood a chance.

Somehow, he had known when he saw her in the bar. It's why he had waited until he was sure she'd left before he went out to his truck.

So much for taking matters into his own hands and putting her safely out of reach. Nope. Fate had stepped in and had made sure they met.

Kismet.

Christian heard the rumble of thunder. With the hurricanes brewing in the gulf, they would likely be getting more rain. Last he checked, the storm was headed toward Florida, but it could turn at the last minute, as they were known to do.

He opened his eyes and pushed away from the doorway. After another look at the floor where he had made love to Ivy, Christian walked out of the shed and up to the house.

As he opened the back door, he spied her boots. He took off his own and went inside. The house was still quiet as everyone slept, but it wouldn't be long now before they woke.

Christian moved silently out of the kitchen and ascended the stairs to his room. He shut his door and immediately started undressing as he made his way to his bathroom.

~ ~ ~

Ivy heard the water turn on next door. She knew it was Christian. She sat cross-legged on the bed as she combed out her wet hair and thought of him taking his shower.

She closed her eyes, imagining her soap-covered hands running over his hard muscles. If only she were with him. She could imagine him pushing her against the shower wall and kissing her. Her lips tingled just thinking about it.

"Stupid, stupid," Ivy said as she opened her eyes and tried to push Christian out of her mind.

It was impossible. She shouldn't still be thinking about him. Yet, how could she not? They were in the same house together. It wasn't like she could leave him behind as she did other men.

What would it be like to have someone like Christian around all the time?

Ivy stopped her thoughts instantly. She knew better than to go down that road. It was better that she was alone. Now more than ever with the Hounds after her. Even if by some miracle she managed to survive them, there was still the threat of her past illness returning hanging over her head.

The worry and fear had taken their toll on her mother, aging her seemingly overnight. Then there were the nights her mother spent at the hospital so Ivy wouldn't be alone.

Even when Ivy was released and had returned home, things had been hard. She couldn't be left alone since she was too weak to do anything herself. Her mother had worked odd jobs just to keep a roof over their heads and pay for a nurse to help care for Ivy.

Ivy could never put someone else through that. She might have been ill, but she'd watched everything unfold from her bed, helpless to do anything for her mother. How many nights had she heard her mother cry herself to sleep?

Ivy dashed away tears of her own. It did no good to cry. She might hate being alone, but she knew it was for the best.

Ivy rose from the bed and grabbed her phone. Stacy had been calling and texting, and Ivy'd had to lie to her friend to keep her from the truth. She hated that. Stacy was one of the few who knew of Ivy's past illness.

She'd told Stacy she was staying with friends, which was about the only thing she hadn't lied about. It's also the only thing that had kept Stacy from trying to see her.

After checking her phone again, Ivy decided to

give her mind a break and play some games on her phone.

It didn't take long before she was absorbed in a game of backgammon. Ivy had no idea how long she played before there was a knock on her door.

"Come in," she said.

The door opened and Davena poked her head inside. Her blond hair was pulled back in a ponytail and she wore her usual smile. "Morning."

"Morning," Ivy replied as she set aside her phone.

"When you get a chance, come downstairs. Beau thinks he has an idea."

"Sure."

"Oh, by the way, here are some clothes," Davena said as she walked into the room and set them on the bed. "You've been in those for a couple of days already."

Ivy laughed and looked down at herself. "Thank you."

"See you in a bit," Davena said and left.

Ivy rose and looked through the assortment of sweats and loungewear. She finally decided on a pair of black sweats and an ash gray tee.

She glanced at herself in the mirror and shrugged before walking out. There was no sound made as she walked barefoot down the stairs to the office where she heard voices.

Ivy stopped when her gaze clashed with Christian's as he once more sat behind the desk. They shared a look before he nodded in greeting.

Hoping no one else saw the awkwardness, Ivy

decided to remain at the entrance. "So, what's this idea?"

Beau shut the book he was reading. "I'll be the first to admit it's not a good one. It's called transference. There is a way that we can transfer your scent to someone else."

"And send the Hell Hounds after them?" she asked, confused. "Absolutely not."

"It may be the only way to save you," Christian said.

Ivy shrugged. "Then I guess I'm going to die because I refuse to give this problem to another innocent."

Vincent asked, "Even if we find someone who deserves it?"

"Even then," she said. She swung her eyes to Christian, expecting him to put up a fight. That's when she realized they were all smiling. "Did I miss something?"

"Just that you're worthy of saving," Beau said and opened the book again.

Ivy came to the conclusion that the Chiassons were a bit off their rockers.

CHAPTER NINE

"You're awfully quiet," Olivia said as she stood by Christian at the desk.

He glanced up from the book he was reading to find that Vincent was with her. Christian shrugged off their words. "I'm busy."

"Since when are you too busy to give us your opinion on anything?" Vincent asked.

Christian released a breath and covertly looked at Ivy, who was standing with Davena at the doorway. "I'm not. I just have nothing to say."

"A first for you." Vin rested a hip on the corner of the desk. "You and Ivy were gone a long time last night."

Christian leaned back in the chair and met Vin's gaze. "What did you expect? For us to start dancing right along with all of you?"

"Y'all do make a cute couple," Olivia said with a smile.

Christian shoved the chair away from the desk and stood. He gathered his books and shouldered his way between Olivia and Vincent to walk from the office.

He needed to be alone, to stop thinking about and looking at Ivy. She clouded his mind so he couldn't sort through things properly. And his family wasn't helping in the least.

Christian took the stairs three at a time and shut himself in his room. He locked it to prevent anyone from barging in then he sat against his headboard and grabbed the book he had been looking through.

~ ~ ~

"What the hell was that?" Vin asked Olivia in a low voice.

She shook her head. "If I didn't know better, I'd say he likes her."

Beau leaned over the desk and whispered, "Because he does."

Vin frowned. Christian? That couldn't be possible. He was so against forming attachments that he went out of his way to ensure no woman would ever want anything lasting with him.

Vincent turned his head to look at Ivy. Then again, Ivy hadn't started out as someone Christian took to his bed. She had been in trouble, and Christian had brought her to the house to keep her safe. Obviously, things had progressed from there.

"What are you thinking?" Olivia asked.

Vin looked down at her. "I think Beau may be right."

Olivia's dark eyes widened. "It would explain why he's so...sensitive about her."

"I honestly never thought Christian would find someone he cared about."

Olivia smiled and rested her hand on his chest. "Things happen for a reason."

Vin frowned then. "If Christian is falling for her, it'll crush him if the Hounds get her."

"We won't let that happen."

No, they wouldn't. It wasn't just about trying to save Ivy, but Christian, as well. Vincent knew his brother would fight against his feelings for Ivy. Vin prayed Ivy was strong enough, smart enough – and cared for Christian enough – to get him over his trepidation.

~ ~ ~

Ivy's eyes burned from staring too long at the computer screen. Hours later, she was still reeling from the "test" she had been put through.

It had made her feel better when Davena told her that Christian hadn't been happy about the test. Davena had assured Ivy that it was only a precaution, but Ivy had the feeling that everyone wanted to make sure she wasn't just worthy of their help, but of being with Christian.

The Chiasson family was a tight-knit group. Ivy

spent half of her time watching their dynamic because it was so foreign. As an only child with one parent, Ivy didn't know what it meant to have so many people looking after her.

The family's love for Christian was visible. Their worry was, as well.

Ivy looked at the ceiling. Christian hadn't left his room since that morning. Lincoln had gone up to try and talk to him. So had Olivia, but neither could get him to come out.

"This isn't normal for Christian," Ivy overheard Ava whisper to Lincoln.

Ivy frowned as she lowered her gaze back to the computer.

Lincoln kissed Ava, then said in a low voice, "It'll be fine in the end. Christian just needs some time."

Time? Time for what? Ivy's mind raced. Surely, she wasn't the culprit. She and Christian had agreed on how things would be. He didn't want any entanglements any more than she did.

Ivy squeezed her eyes closed because she knew that for the lie it was. Why had she found Christian now? Why did he have to be so damn charming and handsome? Why did he have to be so caring and brave?

She opened her eyes and blinked several times. Ivy couldn't look at another website. She closed the laptop and set it aside as she rose and walked out of the office to the front porch.

When she spotted the swing, she smiled and sat. With one leg tucked, she used her other foot to move the swing.

The gray clouds hadn't departed the area. No doubt there was more rain on the way. Ivy braved the mosquitos to have a moment to herself.

The humidity was thick, making her skin sticky and her curls tighten even more. She shoved her hair back and savored the beauty around her. There were live oaks with their thick limbs branching out like gnarled fingers, and crepe myrtles with bright pink blooms still on them.

Christian's truck had been parked with the others off to the side, giving her a clear view of expansive green lawn and the driveway.

How many more days would she get before the Hell Hounds got to her? Was this her last one? If so, why did she even bother talking herself out of whatever feelings had begun to surface for Christian. Who cared if she felt something for him if she was about to die?

Based on everything she had read about the Hell Hounds, if someone did manage to elude them, it wasn't for long. The Hounds always found their scent and took the souls that belonged to Hell.

"Oh, Mom," Ivy murmured.

It was hard for her to even imagine her mother selling her soul. Then again, Ivy had seen how her mother fought to keep her alive. How many times had her mom told her that a parent would do anything for their child?

Ivy didn't completely understand because she didn't have a child of her own, but she knew the depth of her mother's love. Her mother had sacrificed so much for her. It wasn't a stretch to think she would sell her soul for her daughter to become healthy.

Ivy wished her mother had told her so she could've been prepared. But that wasn't her mother. Her mom preferred to keep her worry to herself. Besides, Ivy knew her mom would never have revealed how far she would be willing to go to save Ivy's life.

Movement out of the corner of her eye drew Ivy's attention. She stared at Christian as he walked across the soggy ground to his truck. He opened the tailgate and pulled a large box to him. After he unlocked it, he threw open the lid and rummaged through it.

Ivy watched as he pulled out a crossbow and a set of arrows. Suddenly he stilled, his head swinging to her. Their gazes clashed.

Then he went back to looking in the box. "You shouldn't be out here alone."

"I'm on the porch. It's safe."

"I'd rather you were inside the house."

She raised a brow, giving him her most annoyed expression that he didn't even bother glancing at her to see. "I'd rather be out here."

"Did someone say something to send you outside?" he asked as he shut the lid and relocked the box. Then he closed his tailgate and rested an arm on it as he looked at her.

Damn but his blue eyes could impale her. His black hair was tousled, as if he had been running his fingers through the length.

Ivy realized belatedly that he had asked her a question. "No," she answered. "I'm just not used to so many people around all the time."

"As an only child, I suppose not." He pushed away from the truck and walked to the porch.

He set the crossbow and arrows down and sat on the top step to lean against a column and look at her. Ivy grew self-conscious under his perusal.

"I can't imagine being an only child," Christian said. "Just as I'm sure you can't imagine growing up with four siblings."

Ivy smiled. "I can't. Though, I admit that I like the atmosphere here. The way you all protect each other. You know they'll always be there for you."

"Yeah." He looked down at his hands. "Despite all the tragedies the family has suffered, we do lean on each other. I never thought of that until now." He lifted his eyes to her. "You didn't have anyone to lean on when your mother died."

Ivy shrugged, trying not to feel the same overwhelming sadness that had stayed with her for many months. "I was numb at first. The shock of it all, I guess. I barely remember planning the funeral. I don't think it hit me until a few days after the service when I woke up and walked into the kitchen calling to her." Ivy swallowed, her throat clogged with emotion. "That's when I realized I was alone. The tears I hadn't been able to shed up until that moment were like a dam bursting. I didn't leave the house for days."

"No one should have to suffer something like

that alone."

Ivy hastily wiped away a tear that had escaped. "I got through it."

Christian nodded and looked out over the Chiasson land. "You'll get through this, as well."

"Let's be honest, Christian. Despite all you and your family have done, there's no getting away from the Hell Hounds. This could be my last day."

His head jerked to her, his gaze narrowed and angry. "So you're giving up?"

"I'm not saying that. I get through each day by being realistic. Do I hope something comes of all the research and I get the Hounds off my scent? Yes. But the odds aren't in my favor."

"Sometimes you need to forget reality."

"Reality for me was months in the hospital hooked up to numerous machines that beeped all the time. Reality was taking handfuls of pills three or four times a day to beat whatever was wrong into submission. Reality was not being able to stand on my own or even put on my own clothes. I couldn't feed myself, much less bathe myself. That was reality."

"A reality your mother changed."

Ivy looked away. When she had herself back under control, she met Christian's gaze and stood. "Now my reality is that the Hell Hounds have come to kill me so that they can show my mother my soul before – presumably – it is allowed to go free. Reality is reality, no matter how you look at it."

"Is that right?" he asked and climbed to his

feet. "Hope, Ivy. You need hope. Yes, face your reality, but don't give up. You survived your illness every day because you wished to beat it."

"Don't talk as if you were there and experienced it," she stated angrily and walked to the door.

Before she reached it, she was yanked against Christian's hard chest. His bright blue eyes were alight with some emotion she couldn't place.

"I've experienced you, Ivy Pierce," he murmured before he kissed her.

CHAPTER TEN

Christian had known it was a mistake to pull her against him, but he hadn't been able to stop himself. He'd needed Ivy, like she was a basic ingredient to his survival.

The tightness in his chest loosened when her arms snaked around his neck. He deepened the kiss, his body responding instantly to the heady feel of her.

By the time he ended the kiss, they were both breathing heavily. Christian leaned his forehead against hers.

"Don't give up," he urged.

Ivy smiled and traced his lip with her finger. "I'm not. But you need to be realistic. I might die."

"There's a chance I might die every night I go out hunting," he argued.

She kissed his jaw before she rested her head on his chest. "If the worst happens, it won't be because you didn't do all that you could."

Christian tightened his arms around her. There was a way to save Ivy. There was always a way. He just had to find it.

"I should get back inside and do more research."

Christian didn't let her move. "Not yet. You need to have a bit of downtime."

"You're probably right. I really don't want my last day to be filled with books and computers."

He hated that she was able to be so flippant. It was Ivy's way of coping, but Christian didn't have to like it.

Neither of them spoke about the kiss or the fact they were embracing. Whether she wanted to admit it or not, Ivy didn't want to be alone. Since Christian only wanted to be with her, it worked out perfectly.

Every time he thought about her dying, there was an ache in his chest. It had started small, but it was growing rapidly.

"Do you really never want to fall in love?" she asked into the silence.

Christian wrapped one of her curls around his finger. "My parents were deeply in love. They did everything together. There were many nights I'd wake to hear music downstairs. I'd go to the railing and look down to find them dancing."

"What a beautiful memory."

"It was. I remember barely being able to wait

until I could find such love. Then my mother was killed. I can still hear the bellow that echoed through the bayou when my father found her body. That sound..." he paused and swallowed. "It haunts me to this day. It was like his heart had been ripped from his chest. The desolation, the anguish of that sound was horrible."

Her arms tightened. "I can't even imagine."

"Later that night, he died. He wanted revenge. My father normally had such a cool head when he went hunting. He taught us patience and control, but he had neither after my mother's death."

"You fear you'll be the same."

"I know I will." He kissed the top of Ivy's head. "I know if I ever fall in love it'll be deep. It'll be the kind of love my parents had. I've always known that."

"So you've protected yourself."

He rested his chin atop her head. "I have. Even as I watched my brothers fall in love. It's in my face on a daily basis, but I know what'll happen to them if their women are killed."

"Most people don't understand why we push others away," she said. "They crave being with another, to have that connection. We do, as well, but we know it comes with a price. It's a price some can't pay."

"It's a price some don't want to pay."

Ivy lifted her head from his chest and looked up at him. "You're a good guy, Christian. You have a strong family. You shouldn't push love away if it comes your way. You deserve to be happy."

"And you don't?"

She smiled. "I'm healthy. I fear being that sick again, of being that helpless. It's terrifying. I always figured that I could have one or the other – health or love."

"Your mother sold her soul for you to be well."

"Will it last?" she asked with her brows raised. "What if a miracle happens and we get the Hounds off my scent. Will the Demon of Souls be content with things then? Or will he take away my health?"

"You live in fear."

"And you don't? You fear loving someone so deeply that if they die, you die."

Christian shook his head in denial. "We're talking apples to oranges."

"Says the man who has never been in the hospital for months at a time," she retorted.

Christian stroked a finger down her face. "What if the Hounds leave you alone and you stay healthy?"

"What if love finds you?"

He feared love had already found him. It stood in his arms looking up at him with hazel eyes. "I asked first."

"Those are big ifs, but if it happens, I might have to reevaluate things."

"Me too," he answered. There was no way he could tell her that he felt something for her. Not now. Not after the talk they'd had the night before about not wanting relationships.

She returned her head to his chest. "This is nice."

"Very." Christian closed his eyes and began to pray for a miracle.

~ ~ ~

"I told you," Beau said to the others as they stared out the window watching Christian and Ivy.

Davena elbowed him in the side. "You weren't the only one who saw it."

"I was the only one who said anything."

Lincoln turned away from the window as worry set in. "We better work faster."

"Why?" Vincent asked.

Linc faced the others. "Seeing Christian just now brought back a memory of when we were just boys. Riley was only a baby at the time. Christian told me he couldn't wait to find a love like Mom and Dad had."

"That's not good," Beau said with a frown.

Ava shook her head in confusion. "Why? Wouldn't that be good news?"

Linc looked at everyone in the room. "Christian changed his mind about falling in love after our parents' deaths. If he's falling for Ivy and she dies-"

"It'll crush him like it did Dad," Vincent finished. He slammed his hand into his thigh. "Fuck!"

Olivia took her place on the sofa. "Then we'd better get reading."

"Especially since we don't know how long Davena's spell to mask Ivy from the Hounds will last," Beau said.

Linc returned to the window. Christian and Ivy hadn't moved. He ached for his brother. Here he had a chance at love, and it could very well be snatched from his grasp.

It wasn't right. Christian was the type of man who loved once and loved deeply. Whether he had already fallen for Ivy or was in the process, Lincoln wasn't going to rest until they found a way to save her. His brother deserved happiness.

~ ~ ~

Ivy spent the rest of the afternoon on the porch with Christian. The smell of dinner drifted to them. She snuggled back against him as they lounged on the swing.

Most of the time had been spent in silence. It was a comfortable silence, the kind where each was content to just be with the other.

The few times they had talked had been as he told stories about his family and their exploits. Ivy was amazed she had lived her entire life in Lyons Point and had never heard of the Chiassons.

If she had been well enough to go to school, there was no doubt Christian would've snagged her attention. He was too gorgeous not to.

His question from earlier still rolled around in her mind. If the Hell Hounds released her, and if she remained healthy, would she allow herself to love?

She would only admit it to herself, but she would if it was with Christian. Ivy was able to be herself with him. He made her feel safe and sexy. He inspired wicked thoughts about tearing his clothes off and having her way with him.

It didn't help that she had come to realize he was the type of man who would stay by her side whether she was healthy or not.

"I feel bad that we've been out here so long," she said.

Christian chuckled. "I don't."

"Okay. I don't either," she said with a smile as she tilted her head back to look at him.

He touched her face with the pads of his fingers. "I've enjoyed this."

"I didn't know I needed this. Thank you."

Christian flashed a charming smile. "Any time."

Ivy lowered her head. "We'll have to go in soon."

"No, we don't. We can eat out here."

"Won't that be rude?"

He tugged on her earlobe. "Nope. We can do whatever you want."

"Eating out here sounds fun. If you're sure the others won't be upset."

"They won't," he assured her. "What else do you want to do?"

It began to mist, with the droplets growing in size a few moments later.

"Well, there goes me lying on the ground to look at the stars."

"I'd have taken you to the roof to get you that much closer."

It was such an innocent sentence, but Ivy

smiled in joy because no one had ever done anything like that for her.

"After that?" Christian asked.

Ivy sat up and turned to him. "Will you sleep with me tonight?"

"Absolutely."

She smiled and leaned in to kiss him when a distant howl turned her blood to ice. Ivy froze. Christian jumped up from the swing and pulled her protectively behind him.

"They're a ways off," he said as he scanned the front yard.

"Not that far." They'd found her. Davena's spell had given her a few days, but it looked like her time was up.

Christian took her hand and walked to the door. He yanked the screen open so hard it busted one of the hinges. The front door flew open before he could reach for it.

Lincoln stood in the entrance. He pulled Ivy inside while Christian grabbed his weapon and rushed in the house.

All around her was chaos, as everyone gathered weapons and Davena began to chant, their focus solely on the task at hand. Ivy, however, had eyes for only one person. Christian.

If only she had been able to stop time and have a few more hours with him. She wouldn't have left him after they'd made love. She would've stayed in his arms, watching the rain. Now her choices were about to be taken from her once and for all.

CHAPTER ELEVEN

Christian held his crossbow, knowing that the weapon would do him no good against the Hell Hounds. The Hounds only went after their target – unless someone tried to stop them.

He was going to try and stop them. There was no other choice for him. It wasn't just because he'd promised Ivy he would keep her safe, and it wasn't just his duty as a Chiasson. He would do it because...he loved her.

"Get Ivy to the shed!" Vincent bellowed.

Christian's head swung around to Ivy. He looked into her eyes and saw the stark fear in her hazel depths. She was waiting for his agreement before she did anything.

He rushed to her, grabbing her hand as he walked past and tugged her after him into the kitchen. Beau ran around them and out the back door. He held the screen open, his shotgun pointed up as he looked around.

"Go," he told them.

Ivy stayed next to Christian as they ran from the porch, across the wet grass, and to the shed. Christian whirled around once she was inside to cover Beau as he followed them.

"You should be with Davena," Christian said.

Beau grunted. "She told me you would need me out here."

Christian glanced at Ivy, who stood against one of the large cages. Then he looked at his brother and said in a low voice, "Don't put yourself in the way of the Hounds. You'll get killed, and Davena will be pissed off enough to bring me back from the dead only to dispatch me again for letting you die."

"You think you'll be killed tonight?"

"I'm prepared for it."

Beau nodded slowly. "Does Ivy know?"

"Know what?" Christian asked.

"That you love her."

He looked away. "No."

"Interesting."

Christian returned his gaze to Beau when he heard him dialing someone from his cell phone. He gave his brother a questioning look, but Beau just smiled as he turned the speaker on. After two rings, a male voice answered.

"Kane, we're in a bit of a rush. We need y'all's help."

Their cousin in New Orleans said, "Hang on. Let me get the others." With the phone held away from him, Kane yelled, "Hey! Everyone in Myles's office. Now. It's an emergency!"

Christian looked at Ivy to find her still in the same spot, her arms wrapped around herself. She was doing a good job of holding it together, but it was obvious by the way she shook that she was unraveling.

"We're all here," Kane's voice came through the phone. "What's going on?"

Christian turned his attention to the cell phone. "Hell Hounds."

"You're fucked then," the eldest LaRue brother, Solomon said.

"The woman we're protecting didn't sell her soul," Beau explained.

Christian sighed as the weight of what they were trying settled over him. "It was Ivy's mother. Ten years ago, she sold her soul to help Ivy beat a terrible illness."

"Then what's the problem?" Kane asked.

"Ivy's mother died a year ago. It was ruled a natural death, but we need to know for certain," Beau explained.

There was a string of curses. Then Court said, "We haven't done that much research on the Hounds, but we'll see what we can find."

"We don't have the time," Christian said through clenched teeth.

Beau put his hand on Christian's arm and told the others, "Davena spelled Ivy so that she was hidden from the Hounds. It gave us a few days to do our own investigation, but the spell is wearing off. The Hounds are near."

"You should've called earlier," Solomon said.

Christian hung his head. Their cousins had been a last resort, and it was turning out to be a bust.

"Call Minka."

Christian jerked his head up at the voice. His gaze pinned Beau, but his brother wasn't at all surprised to hear Riley's voice on the other end of the line. "You knew."

He wasn't sure whether to be furious with Beau for keeping their sister's location a secret, or at Riley for staying away.

"Yes, he knew," Riley said. "I asked for some time, Christian, and Beau gave it to me."

Beau shrugged. "It was the least I could do after what we did."

"We'll talk about this later," Riley said, her voice growing stronger as if she walked closer to Kane's phone. "Minka might be able to help."

Christian frowned, wishing his sister and cousins were with him instead of on the phone. "Who the hell is Minka?"

"A witch. A powerful one at that. She might be able to help."

"Then get her on the phone."

"Give me a sec," Riley said.

A moment later, Kane's voice came over the phone. "Riley is calling Minka now. The witch has surprised us in the past. She very well might have the answers you seek."

"Don't get my hopes up," Ivy said.

Christian frowned and walked to her. "I'm asking you not to lose hope."

"I won't have you sacrifice your life or put the lives of your family in jeopardy to protect me. The Hounds will get me one way or another. You and your family have given me a few days. I wouldn't have had that otherwise."

Christian shook his head. "There's a way out of this. We just need to find it."

"Don't lie to her," Solomon's voice said. "It's the worst thing you can do."

Christian ground his teeth together and looked back at Beau and his phone. "I'm not lying. There is a way, and we'll find it."

"Hoodoo," Riley said through the phone. "Minka said to use goofer dust around Ivy."

Beau's forehead furrowed deeply. "That'll only last for so long."

"It'll give Minka time. Do it!" Riley shouted.

Beau tossed his phone at Christian and rushed from the shed. More howls sliced through the night. The Hounds were getting closer. They usually ran in packs of two, but there were instances where three Hounds went after a soul.

Two was bad enough. Three would mean that two would keep them occupied while the third went after Ivy.

Christian hated the fear that filled his belly. Is this what his father had felt the night their mother died, when he couldn't find her?

"Christian?"

Riley's voice pulled him out of his dark thoughts. "Yeah."

"Ivy couldn't be in better hands."

Ivy smiled up at Christian as she replied, "I agree."

Beau stormed back into the shed with Lincoln and Vincent. Christian gave Ivy a quick kiss before he stepped back so Beau could pour the dust around her in a circle.

"It's done," Beau said. "How long do we need to wait, Riley?"

Christian watched his brothers frown while Riley told them it would take as long as it took for Minka to find what she needed.

"She'll work fast," Kane said.

Vincent took a step toward the phone, but Beau put a hand on his chest and shook his head. Vin and Linc exchanged looks, but neither said a word about discovering that Riley was in New Orleans.

"So," Riley said, a smile in her voice. "I can't wait to meet you, Ivy."

Ivy tried to laugh, but her fear was too great. "Same here. I've heard a lot about you."

"Don't believe everything Christian says. He tends to forget things."

Beau snorted. "Always."

Christian glared at Beau. "Hey."

"The truth hurts," Riley said with a laugh.

"Y'all can both kiss my sweet ass." Christian appreciated what Riley was trying to do, but he understood that it was a life or death situation for Ivy.

Ivy's eyes crinkled at the corners as she gazed at him. "If I don't get a chance later, I wanted to thank all of you here and in New Orleans for your help."

"Anytime," the LaRues said in unison.

Vin nodded his head to Ivy. "It's what we do."

"Amen," Linc said as he shot her a wink.

Beau rested his shotgun on his shoulder. "As if we could turn away the one woman who managed to capture Christian's attention."

There was a loud boom as something slammed against the side of the shed. Ivy squatted, her hands over her ears as the Hell Hounds barked incessantly.

"Riley!" Christian bellowed.

"Hang on! Do you hear me? I'm going to be so pissed off if the four of you get yourselves killed!"

Christian set down the phone inside the circle with Ivy and turned around to take his position. He and his brothers fanned out around Ivy with their weapons at the ready.

As suddenly as the Hounds came, the noise ended. The only sound that broke the quiet was Ivy's harsh breaths. No one said a word, not even Riley or the LaRues on the other end of the phone.

The seconds turned to minutes. Finally, Christian said, "Riley?"

"Hang on," their sister said.

Christian could hear her talking to someone else as her voice grew dimmer and dimmer.

"She's on the phone with Minka," Court explained.

Christian prayed that the witch had found something. He couldn't lose Ivy. It would break him as nothing else could.

He realized at that moment that he hadn't been the strong one of the family. He had been the weakest, erecting a barrier around his heart because he had known this day would come.

Just as he knew he wouldn't survive losing Ivy.

"Tell us you have good news, Court," Lincoln said.

Court was silent for a moment. "I can't tell. Riley has her back to us, but she's writing something down."

"You really should've called us sooner," Solomon said. "We could've been there with you."

Christian wished they had called them, but it was too late now. All the research in the world hadn't given them the answers they needed.

Davena, as powerful as she was, didn't know magic like a witch who had been raised using spells did. Without her, however, Ivy wouldn't have had time to prepare. Then again, that might be worse. It might have been better if she hadn't known what was after her.

"Where the fuck are the Hounds?" Christian ground out.

Beau adjusted his rifle. "I like that they stopped their barking."

"I'm with Christian. I'd rather get the show on the road," Linc said.

Vin lowered his machete and turned toward the phone. "Solomon, I'd ask you and the others to continue looking after Riley and to come and get Olivia, Ava, and Davena if the worst happens."

"You have my word," Solomon said.

Christian should have known his brothers would stand with him whether he wanted them to or not. They were Chiassons, defenders of the innocent, slayers of the supernatural.

They were blood, family.

Those ties went too deep for them to let him face the Hounds alone.

CHAPTER TWELVE

To take her mind off of what was happening, Ivy listened to Christian and his brothers. It was only when Vincent asked Solomon to come for their women that she understood.

They planned to put themselves in front of the Hounds to keep her alive.

It boggled her mind. They didn't know her. Sure they protected the parish, but that didn't mean they should sacrifice their lives and leave behind the women they loved just for her.

She was no one. She was worth nothing and left no one behind. The Chiassons, on the other hand, were the one thing that kept the parish safe. They were needed.

Ivy looked at Christian. Her heart ached for what could've been – what should've been. She saw him for what he was – the man who would cherish her, love her, protect her. No longer could she deny what had been building since the moment she'd met him.

Love. The one thing she had kept at arm's length for years.

But it had found her despite her precautions. How sad that she only had a few hours of it. Yet, those few hours had been truly wonderful. To be in the arms of a man who was willing to risk his life for her, a man who always put others before himself.

A man who made love to her with exquisite tenderness and thrilling command. A man who knew the meaning of friendship, family, and love.

Ivy picked up the cell phone. Christian and his brothers began to talk strategy. She took the opportunity offered to her and switched the speaker off.

"Riley?" she whispered into the phone.

Christian's sister answered immediately. "I'm here."

"I know what Christian plans to do. I know that the others will stand with him, but I can't let that happen."

There was a brief pause before Riley asked, "What do you intend?"

"When Christian first brought me here, I didn't understand what your family does. During my time here, I discovered the full extent of things. Christian won't stand down, and neither will your brothers. I can't have them die for me."

"Christian won't let you face them alone," Kane said.

Ivy watched Christian. His black hair was disheveled, his face set in hard lines. "I don't have magic to stop him. But Davena does."

"Oh, God," Riley said in a strangled voice.

Court said, "You'll die, Ivy."

"I'm going to die either way. Why should Christian, Beau, Lincoln, and Vincent join me?"

She knew when no one spoke up that they agreed with her. Now all she needed to do was convince Davena to use magic to stop them.

"I'll call Davena again."

Ivy heard the sadness in Riley's voice. "Thank you. Take care of your brothers, Riley. They regret their actions where you're concerned, but please understand that everything they did was to protect you because they love you so dearly."

Riley sniffed. "I know. The big louts are my world."

"Tell them that, will you?"

Ivy didn't wait for a response. She turned the speaker back on and set the phone down before she stood. When the time came, she would have to act quickly.

The door to the shed flew open. The sliding door behind her began to rattle before it flew open as if a giant had flung it.

Ivy closed her eyes because she knew the Hell Hounds were there, waiting to take her. She sent up a silent prayer that Davena would hurry and set the spell in place to keep Christian from stepping between her and the Hounds.

"They're here," Lincoln said.

Ivy took a deep breath and opened her eyes. Death. That's what stood just a few feet from her. She might not be able to see it, but it was there.

She was thankful the beasts were invisible, or Christian would've already attacked. Not to mention, Ivy couldn't see the Hounds coming for her. It would happen quickly, of that she was certain.

Vincent's machete fell from his hand. He blinked a few times as if disoriented. A moment later, Lincoln's Bowie knives clattered to the floor a heartbeat behind Beau's shotgun.

Christian turned and looked at her, confusion marring his gorgeous face and clouding his eyes.

"It's for the best," Ivy said. "You're needed."

"Ivy," he began as he fought to keep hold of the crossbow.

A tear fell down her face when he lost the battle and the crossbow fell from his lax fingers. He looked from the weapon at his feet to his hands.

"You wanted to save me," Ivy said. "Well, you did. More than you can imagine. Now it's my turn to save you."

She stepped over the line of black dust encircling her and walked to Christian. Ivy cupped his cheek while his blue eyes burned into hers.

"Ivy, please."

"The only way I can do this is knowing that you'll still be around." She forced a smile as her vision swam with tears. "Can't you see, Christian

Chiasson? I fell in love with you."

"Ivy, I-"

She hurried to talk over him because she knew it wouldn't take much for him to change her mind. It was time for her to be strong and do the sacrificing. "This is for you and your family."

Ivy kissed him quickly and walked around him to the door. She looked up and saw Davena, Olivia, and Ava standing on the porch.

"I'm sorry, Ivy. I did the first spell before the one you asked for," Davena said with her hands on the screen surrounding the porch to keep out the mosquitos.

Ivy was confused. "What are you talking about?"

"Minka found a spell that would allow us to see the Hounds," Ava said. "To better fight them."

The night just kept getting better and better. Ivy shrugged. There was no use getting upset over it now. The spell was done, and it had been done to help Christian and his brothers fight.

"I think you're very brave," Olivia said as she wiped at her eyes.

Brave? Not hardly. Ivy just couldn't imagine seeing Christian hurt. That's the only thing that propelled her. Her mother had sold her soul to get Ivy healthy. Christian was willing to die to try and prevent the Hounds from getting her.

"We're going to miss you," Davena said. "You were good for Christian."

Ivy tried to smile but failed. She stepped out of the shed and onto the grass. After a quick glance back at Christian who was watching her, Ivy turned and started walking to the front yard.

Her goal was to get off Chiasson land, but since she had no idea how much land they had, she opted to get as far from the house as she could.

"I'm yours," she told the Hell Hounds. "I'm not going to run anymore. I only ask that you allow me to get far from the house. Please."

She kept walking, her heart pounding in her chest and her body going cold from her blood turning to ice. Every step was a victory, though it took everything she had to remain upright and not collapse where she was.

The tall live oaks stood like silent giants with their thick limbs outstretched as if reaching for her as she passed. The moon was hidden behind the clouds, and the rain was falling lightly now.

It wasn't exactly a beautiful night to die. But when was it ever? Ivy thought back over her life and regretted so much. Was that how most people felt when they knew their time was near?

How much more could she have done and been had she opened herself up to people more? Yes, there would've been heartbreak, but that was part of life. There would also have been joy, happiness, and so many more memories.

Ivy smiled as she thought of Christian. She might regret a lot, but she didn't regret him or their time together. He hadn't let her turn away as she had so many other times.

Christian forced her to see herself. It might have been fear that pushed her to give in to the desire she had for him, but it was love that bound her to him.

Love. The one thing she had thought never to know.

How fate must be laughing at her now.

Ivy squared her shoulders as she crossed over the driveway to another field. She had no idea where she was going, only that it was far away from Christian. He would come looking for her, but he didn't need to find her at the house.

She began to hum to help calm her nerves. The longer it went without the Hell Hounds attacking her, the more frightened she became.

"Mom, I know why you sold your soul now. I wish you hadn't, but I could see myself doing the same for Christian. Your sacrifice gave me a second chance, and I let the past confine me, preventing me from living as you'd hoped I would. I'm sorry for so many things. I hope you're not suffering too much."

The sound of a growl in front of her stopped Ivy in her tracks. Her eyes might be used to the darkness, but she still couldn't see the Hound. And she was immensely grateful.

"You've let me come as far as you will, huh?" she asked the air in front of her. "I guess I owe you my thanks for that concession."

It was the red eyes she saw first. Ivy's mouth fell open when the air shimmered and the Hell Hound became visible. He was huge. His head came to her shoulders, and his body was solid black. He looked like a cross between a Doberman

Pinscher and a Rottweiler.

His ears were pointed, and his teeth were huge as his lips pulled back in a snarl. His paws were easily the size of Christian's hand. The Hound snarled, saliva dripping from his mouth as he continued to growl.

Ivy took a step back and whirled around with a shriek when another Hound snapped his teeth behind her. With her heart in her throat, she counted six Hell Hounds surrounding her.

She lifted her gaze to Christian's house. The porch light was only a faint glow through the trees. She nodded and held out her hands as she closed her eyes.

"I didn't sell my soul. It's not yours to take. It's mine. You might be able to kill me, but you'll never have my soul."

A scream was stopped in Ivy's throat when a Hell Hound pounced on her.

CHAPTER THIRTEEN

Christian didn't take his eyes off the doorway that Ivy had disappeared through. Rage and fear tangled within him until his stomach was in knots.

"Ivy!" he bellowed.

But it did no good. She didn't return.

He could see his brothers fighting the affects of the spell. Suddenly, three figures filled the doorway. And Christian's heart plummeted to his feet.

"Davena, release me. Now," he said through clenched teeth.

Davena walked to Beau and put her hand on his face as Olivia went to Vincent, and Ava stood before Lincoln. "Please don't be angry."

"Drop the spell, honey," Beau said.

The next instant, Christian was able to move. He bent to grab his crossbow as he ran out of the shed shouting Ivy's name. He raced as fast as he could, his lungs burning as he desperately sought to find her.

Christian didn't slow until he reached the empty field a half-mile from their house. He stopped and turned in a circle, not letting the darkness deter him. He spent too many nights in the dark hunting evil.

"Ivy!"

His only answer was the sounds of the bayou. Christian bent over to catch his breath. Behind him, he could hear his brothers running his way.

Christian braced his hands on his knees and squeezed his eyes closed. When he opened them, the clouds broke long enough for the sliver of moon to light the area for a fraction of a second.

Just long enough for Christian to see a glint of something in the grass.

He knelt on one knee and held out his hand behind him. "I need a phone," he said to his brothers as they reached him.

One was quickly placed in his hand. Christian turned on the flashlight app and searched the area.

"What are you looking for?" Vincent asked.

Christian's throat closed with emotion when he lifted a single gold hoop earring. The same ones Ivy had been wearing. He stood and turned to his brothers, showing them the earring.

"Son of a bitch," Beau mumbled as he turned away.

Vincent ran a hand down his face and looked at the ground.

"Let's keep looking," Lincoln said.

Christian enfolded the earring in his hand. "She's gone. I don't hear the Hounds anymore. I lost her, Linc."

He shouldered through his brothers and walked back to the house. Though he could spend an eternity searching the world over for Ivy, he would never find her. She had popped into his life, and departed just as suddenly.

But she'd left her mark upon his heart.

Christian saw the girls standing on the porch, waiting. They said his name, but he was in no mood to talk or listen to Davena's reasoning for doing the spell that had kept him from helping Ivy.

He didn't stop until he was at the doorway of his room. Yet, he couldn't go in. He had to be alone. Christian turned on his heel and walked back downstairs as his brothers were coming in the front door.

"Christian, we need to talk," Vincent said.

He ignored them and strode out the back.

Beau, Lincoln, and Vincent stood on the back porch watching Christian.

"He shouldn't be alone," Beau said.

Linc sighed loudly. "We could go after him, but he would keep eluding us. He needs to be by himself to deal with his grief."

"Ivy's death will kill him from the inside out," Vin said.

Lincoln nodded as Christian vanished into the bayou. "Without a doubt. I just can't believe there wasn't a way to save her."

"Who says we have to stop looking?" Beau

smiled at his brothers. "We all know there are loopholes in all contracts, even the ones set by the Crossroads demons."

Vincent spun and hurried back inside the house. "Get the books, Beau. Linc, call our cousins. It's going to take all of us."

~ ~ ~

Ivy groaned as she rolled onto her side. She ached all over, as if she had been a punching bag for someone. With great effort, she raised herself up on one elbow and opened her eyes.

"What the hell," she mumbled as she found herself on a cold, black stone floor.

A glance showed all four walls also in black. There were no windows, and no door that she could see. Panic began to set in. She sat up and thought of the last thing she had memory of.

"Christian."

That's when she recalled the Hell Hounds. Everything came back in a rush, including the look of the hideous Hounds.

Ivy tried to keep her breathing normal, but the longer she sat there, the more she began to hyperventilate. Was she dead? Was this Hell? Because it certainly couldn't be Heaven.

She scooted back to the wall and set herself in the corner. Wherever she was, it wasn't good. If only Christian were with her. He would know what to do.

Despite her wishing for him, she was glad he

was still with his family. He was alive to defend the
parish as only his family could. She felt good for
having ensured his and his brothers' survival.

Ivy dropped her head back against the wall and
closed her eyes. They'd said the Hounds were only
supposed to kill her, show her to her mother, and
then her soul would go wherever it was supposed
to. Ivy would like to think that was Heaven. She
might not have gone to church every Sunday, but
she hadn't committed murder, stolen, or anything
vile.

Why then hadn't she seen her mother? More
troubling, was how she had gotten to this place?
She didn't remember anything after the Hell
Hound pounced on her. It was fathomable that she
had already been brought before her mother and
killed.

Ivy pinched her arm. She still felt very much
alive. Surely, she would know if she were dead?
Although if she were, she'd missed the pain of it.
Which was a good thing.

"Glad to see you awake."

Ivy's head jerked up as the voice startled her.
She found the woman standing in the middle of the
room. Her long blond hair was a beautiful gold
color. Not a hair was out of place as the length was
pulled over one shoulder in large, loose curls.

Despite the black floor and walls, Ivy was able
to see the woman clearly, as if a light shown on her,
illuminating the black leather jacket that conformed
to her body and the white lace tank beneath.

The woman's long legs were encased in black

leather pants, and she was wearing black stiletto boots. She was smiling when Ivy's gaze returned to her face.

Stunning didn't even begin to describe the woman. She was Charlize Theron beautiful with clear blue eyes, high cheekbones, and perfectly plump lips.

"Like what you see, huh?" the woman asked with a cocky grin.

Ivy stared at her a moment longer. "Who are you?"

"You couldn't begin to pronounce my name. Just call me Liv."

"All right. Liv. Where am I?"

Liv's lips twisted as she shrugged. "You know exactly where you are, Ivy."

"Hell."

Liv nodded.

"Why am I still here?"

Liv raised a blond brow. "That's a bit more complicated."

Ivy used the wall to climb to her feet. "Am I dead?"

"Not yet."

Liv said it with a smile that sent a chill down Ivy's spine. "You're obviously ready to mete out that deed. Why am I still alive?"

"The Chiassons. You have information on them that we'd like."

"Not going to happen."

"Then you'll be down here for a while."

The fear within Ivy was overtaken by anger.

"You can't do that."

"We can do anything we please," Liv said with a confident smile.

"There are many who know the Chiassons. Why are you asking me?"

"Because you fell in love with Christian. You made it so easy. That family has been killing us for centuries, and it's time it stopped."

Ivy squared her shoulders. "You might stop one of them, but not all of them. There are enough that know what the Chiassons do to pick up where they left off if you do manage to kill them."

"Kill them?" Liv asked in a strangled voice. She laughed loud and long. "Oh, sweetie. We're not going to kill them. We're going to turn them to our side."

"Never going to happen."

Liv shrugged as she crossed her arms over her chest and looked Ivy up and down. "Strange things happen when you keep two lovers away from each other. Christian fell hard for you. The longer he goes thinking you're dead, the easier he'll be to turn our way. After all, we have the one thing he wants above anything else."

Ivy covered her mouth with her hand as her stomach revolted. Christian was too strong. He wouldn't fall for what was planned. Not her Christian.

"No."

"You can deny it all you want," Liv said saucily. "We have Christian right where we want him."

Ivy let Liv's words repeat in her head as she

frowned. "You talk as if you've been planning this."

"Well, of course."

"What?"

Liv chuckled and walked to the side to lean against a wall. "You and Christian have been destined for each other since before you were born."

"That's not how it works."

"Denial won't change anything. You humans think you know so much, but in reality, you know nothing. The world runs very differently than you've been led to believe. There are some couples that are destined for each other. Like you and Christian. Then there are some that don't happen until they meet, like Lincoln and Ava."

Ivy was thankful the wall was behind her because her legs were too wobbly to hold her.

"We tried to keep Davena from Beau, but they were another couple fated for each other."

Ivy put her hands over her ears. "Stop talking."

"Is the truth too painful to bear?"

The snarky tone was too much for Ivy. She closed her eyes and thought back to one of the few perfect moments in her life – sitting on the swing with Christian, listening to the rain fall.

"Hold onto your memories while you can," Liv said next to Ivy's ear. "They'll be gone soon enough."

Ivy opened her eyes, but Liv was gone. Ivy slumped to the floor and buried her face in her hands.

CHAPTER FOURTEEN

It was two days after Ivy vanished that Christian returned to the house. He had no intention of staying. He wanted to fill up his backpack with supplies, and then he was leaving.

For good.

"Christian," Davena said as she descended the stairs and saw him in the foyer.

He gave her a nod in greeting, then started up the stairs to his room. She stepped in front of him to halt his passage. Christian released a long breath and then met her gaze.

"I know you're angry with me," Davena began.

He smiled, but there was no humor in it. "You killed her."

"Nothing was going to stop the Hell Hounds from getting her. She wanted to make sure you weren't killed in the process."

"Tell yourself whatever helps you sleep better at night. You did the spell because you didn't want to lose Beau."

Davena's green eyes stared at him coolly. "That's true. Just as Olivia and Ava didn't want to see Vincent and Lincoln die."

"I was willing to die!"

Christian briefly closed his eyes after his outburst and got a handle on his emotions. He pushed past Davena and jogged up the stairs.

"She did it because she loved you," Davena called after him.

He didn't stop, though her words sent a slice of pain through him. Christian yanked open drawers and tossed clothes on the bed. Then he found his backpack and stuffed the clothes inside along with several knives.

Slinging the pack over one shoulder, Christian exited his room and descended the stairs. He paused at the bottom when he spotted his brothers, their women, Kane, and Riley.

He dropped the pack when Riley walked to him. They embraced. Christian held her tight as she sniffed.

"I'm so sorry," she whispered.

Christian closed his eyes. He couldn't talk even if he wanted to. The pain was too raw.

Riley leaned back and held his face between her hands. "We were about to go out looking for you."

"I know the bayou like the back of my hand."

Linc stepped forward. "That's not what she

meant. We're not worried about you out there. We have an idea."

"Riley's idea, actually," Vincent said.

Riley beamed. It was only because of his sister that he didn't walk out right then. He hadn't realized just how much her absence affected them all until she was back in the house.

"Tell me," he urged her.

Riley took his hand and led him into the study. She gave him a little shove to sit on the sofa while the others filed in.

"We've all been looking for a way to get Ivy back," she began.

Christian leaned his forearms on his thighs and dropped his head. "She's gone."

"We're not ready to give up," Beau said. "I can't believe you are."

Christian slowly turned his head to spear his brother with a furious look. "There's no getting anyone back after the Hounds have taken them."

"That's what we thought, as well," Kane said.

Christian refused to allow hope in. He had yet to come to terms with Ivy being gone. The idea that there was a chance he might get her back was too much to bear.

"I lost her once. I can't do it a second time."

Riley sat beside him and draped an arm across his shoulders. "All I'm asking is that you listen to what we've put together. After that, the decision will be yours."

He looked into Riley's blue eyes and couldn't say no. "I'll listen."

"Good." She got to her feet. "When Vin, Linc, and Beau didn't find anything here, we started doing our own search in New Orleans."

Kane grinned. "Except ours wasn't in books."

"Right," Riley smiled as the two looked at each other like conspirators. "We each went to a faction and gathered all the information they had on Hell Hounds."

"As well as what happens if the person who sold their soul dies before the debt is paid," Kane added.

Ava jumped in then. "While they did that, I called in a favor to a Medical Examiner friend and had them look over Ivy's mother's autopsy. There was a high content of licorice root in her system. It can be used for herbal remedies and in tea, but when not used properly, it can cause heart failure. So, our guess was right. She committed suicide."

"Meanwhile, our cousins were putting all their findings together," Lincoln said.

Riley nodded vigorously. "That's when we began to realize that they had one common theme."

"The Hell Hounds have never been stopped by a cloaking spell," Davena said.

Christian frowned as he considered what he had been told. "Then where did the Hounds go for those few days?"

"That was my question," Olivia said.

Christian shook his head. "This doesn't make any sense. They wouldn't just stop coming for Ivy."

"True," Vincent said. "We looked at the date

Ivy was last released from the hospital and never returned. The ten year anniversary was over two months ago."

"If they had come for her soul because of her mother's suicide, they would've come for her two months earlier," Christian said.

Kane folded his arms over his chest as he widened his stance. "Exactly. We found it very odd that the Hounds waited until recently to come for Ivy, and even stranger that they left her alone for a few days."

"It's almost as if they wanted the two of you together," Riley said.

Christian rubbed his eyes with his thumb and forefinger. "This still solves nothing."

"But it proves that the Hounds waited until you and Ivy were in the same location to come after her," Beau pointed out.

Christian lifted his head then. He looked at each of them before he came to Riley. "What is your plan?"

"I came to the conclusion that someone wanted you and Ivy to meet." Riley paused and swallowed, her excitement waning a bit. "The only one who can send the Hell Hounds is the Demon of Souls."

Christian snorted as he leaned back on the sofa. "You think the Demon of Souls wants me?"

"I think he wants our family," Riley corrected him. "Somehow, he knew what would happen if you fell in love and lost that woman."

"So he put Ivy in my path? It could've been any woman."

Lincoln shook his head from the chair next to Christian. "It had to be Ivy. You were so adamant about not falling in love that it would only work if the woman was in need and you came to the rescue."

The longer they talked, the harder it was for Christian to take.

"What we do, battling the supernatural, means we have a lot of enemies," Beau said. "I'm not surprised the Demon of Souls went to such lengths."

Christian sliced his hand through the air to halt any talk. "It doesn't matter. The Hounds killed Ivy."

"Perhaps not," Kane said.

Riley picked up when Kane nodded to her. "Right. We did learn from the Voodoo practitioners that the few instances where the Hounds came for someone like Ivy, they didn't kill them."

Christian got to his feet in a rush. "And you're just now telling me this?" he bellowed.

"You had to know all of it," Vincent said.

Christian ran a hand down his face before he looked back at Riley. "Anything else?"

"We think they're holding Ivy. The others that were taken eventually show up. Well, some of them. It appears that once they're with the demons, they are tricked to sell their soul to save the one who originally sold theirs."

Christian knew Ivy felt guilty for what her mother had done to save her. Would she in turn sell her soul to save her mother?

"We need to find Ivy," he stated.

Vin said, "You realize that means calling for a demon and traveling into Hell to find her?"

"Yes. I also know that few come out after going into Hell. Which is why I'm going alone."

"The hell you are," Lincoln said.

Kane stepped forward. "I'll go with him. You three have ties here. I don't."

"And your brothers?" Beau asked.

Kane glanced at Riley. "They'll understand."

"Ivy went to great lengths to ensure that you three," Riley pointed to Lincoln, Beau, and Vin, "remained to be with your women. Don't screw that up now."

Christian nodded to Kane. "We call the demon tonight. I'm not going to keep Ivy down there any longer than I have to."

"I'll be ready," Kane said.

Christian fell back onto the couch as it all sunk in. He looked to everyone. "Thank you all. It never occurred to me that Ivy could still be alive."

"You were distraught," Olivia said. "It's understandable."

Riley pulled a piece of paper from her back pocket and unfolded it. "Minka also prepared a spell that would help you locate Ivy quickly." She paused and licked her lips. "I want to come with you."

"No," Christian said.

It was Kane who raised a brow. "What none of you realize is that Riley was hunting in Austin the entire time she was in college. She has been hunting with us in New Orleans, as well. She's good. A true Chiasson."

Riley smiled at him, mouthing 'thank you.' Christian realized that the two of them had a friendship both needed. He was glad his sister had found that with Kane when she hadn't from her brothers.

"Having said all of that," Kane continued. "I'm against her joining us."

"Thank God," Vincent mumbled.

Everyone but Riley laughed.

Christian rose and walked to her. He took her hand and waited until she met his gaze. "You have no idea how important you are to this family. You're not just our baby sister. You're the only female. I'd love for you to face this undertaking with me, but you're too precious. Please, Riley, stay here and keep those three in line," Christian said, motioning to their brothers over his shoulder with his thumb.

Riley inhaled and slowly released it as she blinked rapidly. "I'm not giving in because of all those pretty words. I'm agreeing not to go because you asked so nicely."

Christian had a feeling that one day they would all need Riley, just as he knew that his sister would never let them down.

"The demons will figure out quickly enough what we're doing," Beau said.

"And attack us," Vincent added.

Christian rubbed their hands together. "Then

let's make sure we have a grand welcome waiting
for them."

CHAPTER FIFTEEN

Ivy stared at the black walls, her anxiety growing by the moment. How long would she be kept in Hell? She had no intention of telling them anything about the Chiassons that others didn't already know.

It would be the worst kind of betrayal for her to do that to Christian and the others after they'd worked so tirelessly to keep the Hell Hounds away from her.

She owed them so much, especially Christian. No matter what the demons did, she wasn't going to break. She was strong. She could withstand whatever they threw at her.

Ivy must have dozed off because when she opened her eyes, there was someone standing in the far corner. She couldn't make out who it was with the lack of light. She didn't like how the demons could come and go so easily, and she never knew when they would arrive.

With a door, at least she would have a second or two at the sound of opening to prepare.

"Who are you and what do you want?"

The person moved away from the corner, and Ivy's heart stopped when she recognized her mother. She could only stare, taking in her mother's short brown hair and blue eyes.

"Mom?"

"It's me, sweetiepie."

Ivy jumped up and ran to her mother, throwing her arms around her neck and holding tight. The black dress Ivy had buried her in felt smooth beneath her palms. She blinked back tears. "It's so good to see you."

"I know," her mother said and squeezed her tight. "I've missed you so much."

Ivy leaned back and smiled as she took in her mother's face. "How did they let you in here?"

"They told me they had you, and then I was here. Ivy, what is going on? What are you doing in this place?"

She stepped back and shrugged. "Mom, why didn't you tell me you sold your soul?"

"As if," her mother scolded. "Why would I tell you?"

"Why did you do it?"

Her mother rolled her blue eyes. "Why do you think? I had already lost your father and brother. Doctor after doctor couldn't treat you. They had you on so many medications that I knew weren't good for you. You were dying. Slowly. I saw it month after month, year after year. I couldn't lose you, too."

"You shouldn't be in Hell," Ivy said and felt a tear fall on her cheek.

Her mother smiled sadly. "One day, you'll understand the lengths a parent will go to in order to help their children. My soul was an easy price to pay, knowing that you would be healthy."

Ivy nodded because she couldn't get any words out. It took her a few moments to push the tears aside. "How did the demon find you?"

"I was coming out of the hospital chapel after another set of prayers." Her mother looked away, sadness contorting her face. "He approached me then, but I walked right past him."

Ivy wrapped her arms around her middle. There was so much to know and say, and now was the time for her to listen. She could ask questions later.

"I saw him for three consecutive days after," her mother continued. "Two days later, we finally got results back on another round of testing the hospital had performed, and just like before, the doctors had no clue what was wrong with you. If they couldn't diagnose it, they couldn't treat it."

Ivy had heard that far too many times from baffled doctors who shuffled her off to someone else.

"You'd already spent so many years watching life from your bed in the hospital and at home. You deserved a life instead of watching others' on TV. I decided then that I would talk to the demon. It took me another two days before I found him again. This time, I approached him."

Ivy waited for her mother to continue. When she didn't, Ivy urged, "And?"

"I was desperate to heal you. I accepted his offer for my soul for your instant recovery. I was told I would have ten years with you before my soul would be claimed."

All this Ivy knew, but to hear it from her mother. It was so...wrong. "You died a year too soon."

"I did."

"That doesn't normally happen."

She shrugged her shoulders. "It does sometimes."

"You killed yourself, didn't you?"

For a long silent minute, her mother simply stared at her. "Yes. I didn't want to chance you being around when the Hell Hounds came for me."

"Did you know that when a person who has sold their soul commits suicide, the Hell Hounds come for the one that was saved?"

Her mother blinked, a shocked expression crossing her face. "No."

"Yes." Ivy tucked a curl that kept falling in her eyes behind her ear.

"How did you figure all this out?"

Ivy thought of Christian. "I had some help from people who fight demons and the like."

"Really? Who are these people?"

She quickly changed the subject to get it off

Christian. "The Hounds found me and brought me here."

"What happens now?"

"After I see you, they kill me."

Her mother put her hands over her mouth and shook her head. "I won't let that happen."

"It's too late." Ivy wasn't sure why she didn't want to tell her mother about Christian or the demons interest in the Chiassons. It was jut a gut feeling, and Ivy didn't fight it.

"What about the people who told you of the Hell Hounds? Will they come to help you?"

Ivy shrugged. "I don't think so."

"What are their names? Perhaps we can find a way out?"

That's when Ivy knew that she wasn't talking to her mother. The woman who had sat beside her hospital bed for months at a time would never care more about learning a name than finding a way to get Ivy out.

"There's no leaving Hell," Ivy said.

Her mother looked around the room. "There's always a way. We need to learn what we have that can be used to bribe the demons."

"You sold your soul," Ivy said in a flat tone. "There isn't a demon here who would release you."

"Ivy," her mother admonished. "I can't believe you would say something so cruel. I sold my soul for you."

Ivy smiled, the tears gathering quickly. "My mother would never say such a thing to me. She would never make me feel guilty for my illness or for her selling her soul."

Her mother smiled maliciously. Then the form changed and it was once more Liv. "Well, aren't you the smart one? I'll have to be more careful in the future."

"As if I would ever believe I was talking to my mother after this," Ivy snapped.

Liv raised a blond brow. "Oh, you poor thing. You had no idea that it wasn't your mother at first, did you?"

For the first time in her life, Ivy wanted to hit someone. "Go away."

"We're not nearly done," Liv said in a sickeningly sweet voice. "We're just getting started."

Ivy felt her stomach churn when she heard a scream filled with pain, and then recognized her mother's voice begging for it to stop.

"That's what happens when you sell your soul," Liv said. "That soul is ours. To do with whatever we want. And we do love our torture."

"Threaten me all you want."

"You?" Liv asked with a laugh. "Why would we do that when we have your mother?"

~ ~ ~

The sun had barely sunk into the horizon before Christian stood at a crossroads. He recited the words his family had gathered generations ago to call certain demons.

Christian didn't have long to wait before a

young man of Italian descent appeared before him in a suit. Christian looked into his soulless eyes and fought back a glare of disdain.

The demon looked at Christian, then spoke with a heavy Italian accent. "Christian Chiasson. I never expected you to call to me. You come to sell your soul?"

"I would never."

"Not even to save your precious Ivy?"

Christian ground his teeth together to hold back his temper. He forced a smile then. "I'll save her. Just not by selling my soul."

The demon laughed and put one hand in his pants pocket. "So conceited. How many of your family have to die before you all realize we'll win."

"If it were so set in stone, you wouldn't still be trying to kill us."

"Good and evil. We will battle until the end of time."

Christian looked past the demon to see Kane rise up from the ditch. "With good gaining ground at every turn."

"Ne-" The demon spun at the last minute as he heard Kane. "What are y-"

His words were cut off as Kane plunged a dagger blessed by the church into the demon's heart. The demon jerked, his face going blank with surprise.

Christian rushed to the demon and grabbed hold of his arm as the earth opened up. It took everything they had to keep a grip on the demon as his human form fell away and his demon form began to burn from the inside out.

"We better reach the bottom soon!" Kane yelled over the demon's screams as they fell.

Christian's hands began to burn. If they held on any longer, they would be killed. "Let go!"

They released the demon and tumbled through the darkness. Christian was the first to hit the bottom. He landed on his stomach. A second later, there was a thud as Kane landed.

Christian opened his eyes to the darkened corridor. He turned his head to see Kane on his back, moaning in pain. He knew exactly how his cousin felt. His entire body ached as if it had just fallen twenty stories, which they probably had.

They didn't have time to stay there. They had to get moving before the demons found them. With great effort, Christian got to his hands and knees and crawled to Kane.

"Come on," he said hoarsely, his head pounding so fiercely he wanted to throw up.

Kane rolled toward Christian. They used each other to climb to their feet before rocking unsteadily.

"Let's hope we don't meet a demon soon," Kane whispered. "I think I broke my arm in the fall."

Christian was sure he had a concussion, but there was no time to think about that now. He had to find Ivy. Davena had done the tracking spell to find Ivy before they'd called the demon. It just needed to kick in.

"We've no idea how big Hell is," Christian said.

Kane chuckled and looked at him. "Copious demons. Abundant souls trapped. This place will be huge."

"Why can't anything be easy," he griped.

Kane's lips twisted in annoyance. "And why does everything have to be dark?"

Christian was opening his mouth when he felt a pull to the right. He looked in the direction of the tug as it grew stronger.

"I feel it, too," Kane said. "Let's go find Ivy."

For the first time in days, Christian smiled. Ivy was close.

CHAPTER SIXTEEN

Christian plastered himself against a wall after glancing around the corner and seeing two demons coming his way. He nodded to Kane, who stood beside him, knife at the ready.

Christian had his own blade, and as soon as the demons turned the corner, he and Kane killed them. That made eight they had killed since coming to Hell. He would gladly gut thousands more if it meant he could find Ivy.

The screams were the worst to hear. The pain and suffering echoed through the halls. It was music to the demons, but all Christian wanted was for it to stop.

They had been walking the halls for thirty minutes. With every step, the pull became stronger as he got closer to Ivy. Yet, the farther they went, the more demons they encountered.

Neither he nor Kane mentioned it, but both knew the chances of either of them leaving Hell were slim.

They hurried to the next turn. Kane reached it first and peeked around the corner. He leaned back and inhaled deeply before looking Christian's way.

Their gazes locked. Then Kane said, "Don't worry. The others will be fine."

Christian glanced at the blade in his hand. "Their distraction isn't working as I had hoped it would. Then again, I'm not all fired up about them surrounded by demons."

"It's what we do," Kane said with a grin.

"That it is."

Kane glanced around the corner again. "There are four of them. Ready?"

Christian was nodding when there was suddenly shouting and a commotion. The uproar grew, and through all the voices suddenly coming from around the corner, he heard one name – Chiasson.

Kane took another look and let out a string of curses. "There must be over two dozen now."

They couldn't turn away. Ivy was near. But neither could they go forward and face so many with just the two of them.

"Ideas?" Kane asked.

Christian gripped the handle of the knife tightly. "The distraction from the others is working. Let's hope that means the demons will leave soon."

The voices grew. Kane motioned Christian back to a doorway where they quickly hid just as the demons rushed passed. It wasn't the only hallway where the demons had gathered.

Kane whistled low after the demons passed. "We need to watch Riley if she survives this. Her idea to trap a second demon after us and torture him was smart, but it's moves like that that'll get her killed."

"Don't I know it," Christian mumbled.

It seemed to take forever for the halls to grow quiet. Christian and Kane waited another few minutes before they snuck out of their hiding place and once more followed the pull they had to Ivy.

~ ~ ~

Ivy heard the loud, angry voices seeming to come at her from everywhere. Liv's gloating was erased as she listened to the demon speak, something Ivy couldn't understand.

She desperately wanted to ask Liv what was going on, but her curiosity wasn't great enough to get the demon's attention back on her. Instead, Ivy watched Liv's face twist with fury.

Liv slid her gaze to Ivy and closed the distance between them. She poked Ivy hard in the shoulder. "The Chiassons will die tonight. They think they're strong enough to trap a demon and torture him. We'll show them who has the stronger numbers."

And then Liv was gone.

Ivy slumped forward. She was delighted the demon was gone, but she began to worry about Christian. What was he thinking, trapping a demon? From what she'd learned while staying with them, the Chiassons didn't torture. They killed.

So what the hell was going on?

Ivy walked around the square room and began to run her hands along the walls in an effort to find a way out. There had to be a doorway. She just needed to find it.

She went around the room twice before she slammed her balled fist into the wall and screamed her frustration. Christian was fighting demons, not having any idea that those demons were trying to learn anything they could to take the Chiassons down.

"Christian," she whispered.

This trap the demons had set was too good. None of them had thought she was being tracked by the Hell Hounds for anything other than her mother dying before the ten years was up.

If only Ivy could let Christian know somehow. This was a nightmare that felt as if it would never end. The despair was overwhelming, but it was nothing compared to the stark fear that Christian might die.

While her mother may have been devout in her religion, Ivy wasn't. No matter how many times she prayed to find out what was wrong so she could be healed, nothing ever came of it.

As a child, her first thought was that she hadn't prayed properly. That's when she asked her mother if the priest could come to their house on occasion. Not even that seemed to help.

No matter how many times Ivy prayed, God didn't seem to be listening. As the years wore on, she prayed less and less. After she was healed, Ivy only went to church with her mother because she didn't want to tell her mom that she didn't believe in God anymore.

But now...now that she knew there were demons, there also had to be a God.

Ivy pressed her cheek against the wall and closed her eyes. "If you're listening, I need your help. Please. I know I turned away from you for many years, and I probably have no right to ask anything of you now. But I am. I'm in Hell, trapped by demons that want the Chiassons. Christian and his family are good people. They protect others. They don't deserve what the demons have planned. If there is a way to let Christian know they're about to be swarmed by demons, please tell them."

Ivy sniffed and pushed away from the wall. She tried to remain calm for all of a minute, and then she snapped.

She slammed her hands against the wall and began to shout until her throat was hoarse. "Let me out! Let me out!"

"Ivy!"

She paused in her screaming. That was Christian's voice she heard in her mind. Was she breaking that quickly? She had to be stronger.

"Ivy?"

She squeezed her eyes closed. He wasn't there. That sexy voice wasn't close. It was all a trick from the demons, or her mind – or both.

"Ivy Pierce, turn around and look at me!" Christian demanded.

She laughed then. How quickly she had gone insane to believe that Christian was really there. She slowly turned and looked at the wall where his voice had come from.

"Go away, demon! I won't be tricked by you again," she declared.

"Dammit, Ivy. It's really me. I came to find you."

Ivy threw back her head and laughed, the sound hollow to her own ears. "Right. Just as you were my mother not that long ago while trying to find out all you could about Christian and his family. Not going to happen, bitch."

The silence that followed felt like a punch in her gut.

"Ivy, sweetheart," Christian's voice said in a low tone. "I'm standing right here. See me. See that I'm real."

She threw her hands out. "You're not here!"

"Listen to my voice," he said calmly. "Track it to where I am. Look past the walls the demons erected in your mind and understand that there is nothing holding you."

Nothing holding her? What did that mean? Did he actually mean there weren't walls around her? Ivy fisted her hands and shook her head.

The demons and their tricks. If they could make her think she was talking to her mother one minute and it be the demon the next, why couldn't they also make her think she was locked in a room?

"That's it," Christian said in encouragement. "You can do this, Ivy."

She closed her eyes and concentrated on Christian's voice. Even if he was a figment of her imagination, he was calm in a storm of chaos. She would listen to him only because he gave her the confidence to face what was before her.

When she opened her eyes, the walls weren't as thick as before. She looked at the one she had been banging on and tried to hit it again, only to have her hand go through the stones.

As if that was all her mind needed, the walls vanished.

She turned in a circle to find herself in a large room with corridors leading in different directions. It wasn't until she saw Christian and another man beside him that she felt her knees weaken.

Ivy wanted to run to Christian, but she kept still for fear it was a demon again.

Christian smiled widely. "This is Kane," he said and motioned to his cousin. "He came to help me find you."

"You can't be in Hell," Ivy said.

Christian shrugged. "It seems I would walk through Hell itself for you, Ivy Pierce."

She shook her head. "I've been tricked before. This isn't you."

Kane held up a large knife that dripped with something dark and kicked at a burning body at his feet. "Trust me, Ivy. It's us. We went through a lot of pain to get here, and have killed many demons. If we don't get out of here soon, the demons will figure out what's going on."

Ivy noticed Christian had his own blade. She looked into his face and gave him a sad smile. "Make me believe it's you."

In two strides, he was before her, yanking her against him and kissing her.

No one else could kiss like Christian Chiasson. Ivy wrapped her arms around his neck and returned his kiss, overjoyed that it was really him.

She ended the kiss and hugged him. "It's really you."

"I tried to tell you, sweetheart. Now, are you ready to get out of here?"

"Please," she said as she released him.

Christian entwined his fingers with hers. "Let's go."

Together, the three of them ran down first one hallway and then another and another. They began to blur together, and Ivy soon got turned around.

"Where are we going?" she asked.

It was Kane who said, "Back where we landed."

Ivy wanted to ask how they were going to get home, but she trusted Christian to have already thought of that. He wasn't the sort to go into a place without having a way home.

They rounded another corner when Christian said, "It's just up ahead."

Before they could reach it, six demons appeared before them, led by Liv.

Ivy took the knife from Christian and rushed Liv. The demon never saw the blade until it plunged into her heart. Christian grabbed Ivy and the blade and spun them around. He bent over her while Kane battled two demons.

And then suddenly there were no more sounds of battle. Ivy lifted her head and blinked at the bright light to find Davena sitting in the middle of the living room with candles all around her.

Davena smiled at them. "It's good to have you home, Ivy."

Kane and Christian jumped up and ran out the front door. Ivy moved slower, but when she stood on the porch and saw the demons and the Chiassons fighting them, Ivy couldn't breathe.

With Christian and Kane joining in the fray, it was enough to allow Olivia and Ava to get back to the house. Ivy couldn't take her eyes off Christian.

He was right in the middle of it all, fighting demon after demon as they fought to get at him.

"Davena!" Beau shouted.

With a few simple words, the demons burst into flames. Their screams filled the air for a few seconds before they disappeared.

Ivy ran down the steps and straight into Christian's arms. "You came for me."

"I didn't lie when I said I would walk through Hell for you. I love you, Ivy Pierce. Don't ever leave me again."

"I wouldn't dream of it," she said as she pulled his head down for a kiss. "How can I when I love you so?"

EPILOGUE

A week later...

Ivy sat in Christian's arms on the swing. The Chiasson house was getting very crowded, even though Kane returned to New Orleans after the demon battle. Riley remained, but she was packing her bags to return.

"This isn't going to be good," Christian said when voices from inside drifted out.

Ivy patted his leg. "Vin needs to let her go."

"He's right though. Riley belongs here. We need her."

"And she needs New Orleans right now. Give her time. She'll return."

Christian's arms tightened around her. "I hope you're right."

"I'm always right."

"Oh, really?" he asked with a laugh as he nuzzled her neck.

Ivy nodded. "Get used to it."

"I've already gotten used to quite a lot of things. Like going to bed with you and making love all night." He turned her so that she could look at him. "And watching the morning sun come through the window to touch your face before you wake up and give me a smile."

She touched his cheek. "I never wanted to love, but now that I do, I'm surprised at how fast it grows. I didn't think it was possible to love you more than I did yesterday, but I do."

"I know," he said and kissed her.

She turned so that she straddled his lap and began to tug his shirt up. They were interrupted by the sound of a car approaching.

"Marshall," Christian said.

Ivy got off his lap and straightened her clothes. Christian stood at the top of the porch steps and waited for the patrol car to park.

A tall man with short black hair got out of the car and put on his cowboy hat. He wore jeans, a button down shirt, and boots, and had a holster slung around his hips.

"You look like hell," Christian said with a smile. He held out his hand for Ivy who took it and stood beside him.

Marshall walked to the front of his car and leaned back against it. He crossed one ankle over the other and hooked his thumbs in his pants pockets. "I feel it. I never thought I would get the US Marshalls out of my office."

"Did they find anything?"

"No, but that huge burst of flames the other week didn't help matters. I had calls coming in from everywhere." Marshall pinned Christian with his steel gray eyes. "A little heads-up would've been nice."

Christian laughed and walked down the steps, pulling Ivy with him. "Yeah, we'll work on that. Sheriff Marshall Ducet, let me introduce Ivy Pierce."

Marshall touched the brim of his hat. "Ma'am." He blinked and looked closer at Ivy before his smile widened as his gaze moved to Christian. "I knew you had a thing for her. You couldn't stop looking at her at the bar."

"I know," Ivy said as she leaned into Christian. "I couldn't stop looking either. The demons said we were fated to be together."

Marshall's brows raised. "Demons? Really? But being fated, I guess that makes things easier."

"Fated or not, Ivy is meant to be mine," Christian said as he gazed down at her.

"I'm going to have to stop coming here," Marshall said when they kissed. "Couples everywhere. Looks like my pool partner is gone. There goes my Friday nights."

At that moment, the screen door flew open as Riley walked out of the house with her bag over her shoulder. She walked to her Jeep and yanked open the door, even as Vincent and Lincoln were calling her name.

Ivy and Christian turned to see Beau watching it all with a smile and an arm around Davena. Olivia and Ava were trying in vain to call their men back.

Riley had known it wasn't going to be easy to leave again, but she had to do it. Not because she wanted to, but to prove to everyone – including herself – that she was capable of doing it.

"It's not for good," Riley said, quieting her two eldest brothers instantly. She took a deep breath. "I'll be back."

"When?" Vincent demanded.

She cocked her head and gave him a stern look. "I'm an adult. I have been for awhile, but none of you were able to see it. I've made a life in New Orleans."

"Delphine is there," Lincoln said.

As if she didn't know that. Riley started to say something, but the words evaporated when she saw the sheriff's car and the hunk leaning back against the hood. His silver-gray eyes watched her fervently. His black hat covered most of his hair, but there was enough showing at the sides and back with a bit of wave to it that had Riley itching to take the hat off him.

"It's just Marshall," Vincent said. "What were you going to say?"

Was she going to say something? For the life of her, Riley couldn't remember. Then all thought fled when Marshall tilted his hat back enough that she got a good look at his face.

Lean and rugged. He had a shadow of a beard

that accentuated his amazing jawline and entirely too full lips.

He pushed off the car and stood straight. Lord, was he ever tall. His jeans fit his long legs perfectly, and his white button down shirt with the sleeves rolled above his elbows emphasized his wide shoulders and broad chest.

"Riley!"

She jerked at Lincoln's voice. Riley glared at them again. "I'm just a few hours away. You know where I am now. There's no cause for any worry."

"Are you kidding me?" Vincent asked in shock.

"Vin, careful now," Olivia cautioned him.

Riley nodded to Olivia. "You need to listen to her. You're walking dangerous ground here telling me I can't leave."

"We're better with you here," Lincoln said.

Vin turned and looked at Beau and Christian. "And why the hell aren't you two trying to keep her here?"

"Because she's happy in New Orleans," Beau said. "I saw that firsthand. Besides, she's good for Kane."

When Vincent turned his attention to Christian, he merely shrugged. "I'm sorry, Vin. Did you say something? I was kissing my woman."

Ivy giggled and kissed him again.

Riley shook her head with a smile. "I never thought I would see the day that my brothers found love, but each of you have. Vin, you and Olivia are about to be married. Lincoln and Ava aren't far behind. It won't be long after that before

Beau and Davena and Christian and Ivy are also married. We can't all live in the house."

"There's someone in New Orleans, isn't there?" Lincoln asked.

Riley glanced at Marshall to find a small frown on the man's face. She waved away Lincoln's words. "Maybe. Maybe not. It doesn't matter. I'll call y'all when I get there."

She got in her truck and closed the door before there could be any more arguments. Riley started the Wrangler and put it in reverse when she noticed that Marshall had taken a few steps toward her.

He was handsome. Too handsome. A man like that would break her heart, and she had had enough of that.

Riley backed up before she put the truck in drive and started down the long driveway. She looked in the rearview to find everyone was going back inside except for Marshall.

He stood staring after her.

Look for the next story in the Chiasson series with their cousins, the LaRues in MOON STRUCK – Coming October 2015!

Until then, read on for the sneak peek at SOUL SCORCHED, the sixth book in the Dark King series...

Dreagan Industries

Edinburgh, Scotland

Darcy sat straight up in bed, her chest heaving from her gasping breaths. She clawed at the hair that clung to her face with her sweat and blinked several times to make sure the dragon who had been bearing down on her with its mouth open wasn't real.

She hunched over and buried her face in her hands, her entire body shaking. It was the same dream from two days earlier. For the past month, the dream kept recurring every few days. There was no rhyme or reason to when the dreams came or when they didn't. All Darcy knew was that the dragon was after her.

She lifted her face to peek out her window. Dawn had arrived. She took several deep breaths before she threw off the covers and rose to walk to the bathroom. After a quick shower, she pinned up her hair and pulled on a sweater, jeans, and boots before she walked to the kitchen of her flat. A quick inhale of the smell of coffee brought some semblance of a smile to her face.

Darcy poured the dark liquid into a tall thermal container and screwed on the top. She put on her coat and pulled her purse over her head, settling it across her body. As she made her way to the door, she grabbed an apple from the basket.

The few blocks she walked to work was done slowly. She wasn't in a mad dash like others in the city heading to their corporate jobs.

By the time she reached the black door of her shop, she had finished the apple. Darcy opened the door and stepped inside. She shut and locked the door behind her. It was a few hours yet before she would officially open, but she always came in early.

She walked past the round table painted black set in the middle of the floor. All around the front of the small store were decorations that people expected to see like a crystal ball and crystals of various sizes and colors hanging from the ceiling.

Simple was best, and it was what she liked. Darcy didn't put up any brightly lit signs announcing that she read palms. People always found her, and her clients returned again and again.

Although she could read palms anywhere, she preferred the place kept darkened. So the lights were dimmed and candles lit. The walls were painted a dark purple, and the hardwood floor was covered with black rugs of various sizes and shapes.

She walked through two sets of dark hanging

curtains to the back of the store that held boxes of different tarot cards, runes stones, and books about reading the tarots and runes, as well as palm reading. She made the bulk of her money from her clients, but she made a nice chunk with her online sales.

This was the place she called her mini-warehouse because of all the boxes. She had a small desk that housed her computer and printer. All her shipping supplies were in cabinets hanging on the wall above her desk, which meant it was as neat as it was going to get.

Darcy hung her purse on the coatrack, and her coat soon followed. She tapped a key on the computer keyboard to wake it up as she walked to the back door.

She quickly threw open the door and sighed. This was the place she craved to be. This is what the money from her palm readings and online sales allowed her. She was finally able to find some semblance of comfort since the dream woke her.

The conservatory was long and narrow, going back as far as it could until it reached the building behind hers. Darcy took a deep breath, the air filled with the fragrance of dozens of flowers. This is what calmed her. It was the place she went to ease her mind and find peace that eluded her out in the world of crazies.

Darcy didn't bother with gloves. She pushed the sleeves of her sweater up her arms and put on the apron that held the tools she would need to tend to her flowers.

She looked over the tables of plants to the planters in the back that held the tallest flowers. Then she walked to the table to her left.

One by one Darcy lovingly touched their leaves and inhaled the fragrant flowers while she checked the soil and pruned as needed. She went down the first row, moving to her right until she reached the end.

She was at the middle table working her way back to the front when she noticed the Scottish primrose she had planted from a seed. It had sprouted well enough, but yesterday it began to look as if it was struggling to live.

Darcy leaned close and cupped her hands around it. She let her magic fill her before she released a small portion of it through her fingers into the plant.

She didn't normally use her magic with her plants, but the primrose had been a gift from her sister. It had taken her six years to get up the courage to plant it, and now that she had, she didn't want it to die.

As she watched the leaves of the flower begin to brighten, she dropped her hands to her side and straightened. She didn't need to turn around to know who had come into the area. There was only one person who would dare to intrude upon her privacy.

"I honestly didn't expect to see you again."

"And I didna expect to see you cheating by using your magic," came the masculine reply in a deep, soft English accent.

Darcy turned and faced the man who had first walked into her shop three years earlier. She looked over his long black hair that hung loose about his shoulders to his gold eyes. As usual, he was in a dark suit, the crisp white shirt beneath the jacket left open at the collar.

Ulrik.

Her first foray into a world she hadn't known existed—the Dragon Kings.

Thank you for reading **Wild FLAME**. I hope you enjoyed it! If you liked this book – or any of my other releases – please consider rating the book at the online retailer of your choice. Your ratings and reviews help other readers find new favorites, and of course there is no better or more appreciated support for an author than word of mouth recommendations from happy readers. Thanks again for your interest in my books!

Donna Grant

www.DonnaGrant.com

ABOUT THE AUTHOR

New York Times and *USA Today* bestselling author Donna Grant has been praised for her "totally addictive" and "unique and sensual" stories. She's written more than thirty novels spanning multiple genres of romance including the bestselling Dark King series featuring immortal Highlander shape shifting dragons who are daring, untamed, and seductive. She lives with her two children, two dogs, and four cats in Texas.

Connect online at:

www.DonnaGrant.com

www.facebook.com/AuthorDonnaGrant

www.twitter.com/donna_grant

www.goodreads.com/donna_grant/

Never miss a new book
From Donna Grant!

Sign up for Donna's email newsletter at
www.DonnaGrant.com

Be the first to get notified of new releases and be eligible for special subscribers-only exclusive content and giveaways. Sign up today!